Bella Broomstick
MIDNIGHT MAGIC

D0226759
904 000 00624620

Also by Lou Kuenzler

Bella Broomstick
School Spells

Bella Broomstick
Halloween Havoc

Bella Broomstick
Strictly Spells

Princess Disgrace:
First Term at Tall Towers

Princess Disgrace:
Second Term at Tall Towers

The Incredible Shrinking Girl:
Definitely Needs a Dog

The Incredible Shrinking Girl:
is Totally Famous

Bella Broomstick

MIDNIGHT MAGIC

LOU KUENZLER

ILLUSTRATED BY
KYAN CHENG

SCHOLASTIC

Scholastic Children's Books
An imprint of Scholastic Ltd
Euston House, 24 Eversholt Street, London, NW1 1DB, UK
Registered office: Westfield Road, Southam, Warwickshire, CV47 0RA
SCHOLASTIC and associated logos are trademarks and/or
registered trademarks of Scholastic Inc.

First published in the UK by Scholastic Ltd, 2018

Text copyright © Lou Kuenzler, 2018
Inside Illustrations copyright © Kyan Cheng, 2018
Cover Illustration copyright © Nicola Slater, 2018

The right of Lou Kuenzler and Kyan Cheng to be identified as the
author and illustrator of this work has been asserted by them.

ISBN 978 1407 18670 2

A CIP catalogue record for this book
is available from the British Library.

All rights reserved.
This book is sold subject to the condition that it shall not,
by way of trade or otherwise, be lent, hired out or otherwise circulated in
any form of binding or cover other than that in which it is published. No
part of this publication may be reproduced, stored in a retrieval system,
or transmitted in any form or by any means (electronic, mechanical,
photocopying, recording or otherwise) without prior
written permission of Scholastic Limited.

Printed by CPI Group (UK) Ltd, Croydon, CR0 4YY
Papers used by Scholastic Children's Books are made
from wood grown in sustainable forests.

This ... ... written, places, incidents
and ... ... are products of the author's imagination or are used
fic... ... ... to actual people, living or dead,
... ... events or locales is entirely coincidental.

... ...tic.co.uk

Waltham Forest Libraries	
904 000 00624520	
Askews & Holts	10-Aug-2018
STO	£5.99
5795408	⌐

Chapter One

It was a bright and beautiful Saturday morning – the first day of our spring half-term break. I had just stepped into the front garden to enjoy the sun, when I saw my rich neighbour, Piers Seymour, coming out of his enormous house next door.

"Hello, Piers! Are you going somewhere?" I asked. He was rolling along a huge, shiny silver suitcase on wheels.

"Oh, hi, Bella!" he called, waving at me

over the fence. "We're off on a little holiday.
We're just going to the airport now!"

"The airport?" I gasped. "You mean . . .
you're going to *fly . . . in a real, actual
plane*?" I would love to take a trip in
aeroplane, especially if I was going on
holiday somewhere, but I've never had
the chance.

"Of course, in a plane," snorted Piers.
"How else are we going to fly across the

ocean? We can't just hop on a broomstick like you would!"

"Shh!" I whispered, glancing over my shoulder to check that no one else had heard him.

You see, Piers knows my secret. He knows that I am a witch.

I've only been living here at Honeysuckle Cottage with my lovely foster parents for about half a year. Before that, I was raised in the Magic Realm by my horrible Aunt Hemlock, who is a witch too. She has proper, wobbly, green witchy warts on the end of her nose and everything! I don't – I look just like an ordinary girl. I don't even wear a pointy hat, and it's been *ages* since I turned anybody into a frog.

"Oh, Piers, you are lucky. I wish I was going somewhere in an aeroplane," I said, looking up at a long white vapour trail in the blue sky above our heads.

Even though I grew up in the Magic Realm with sorcery and spells all around me, I'm still amazed by how clever inventions here in the Person World are. Things like planes and helicopters – or roll-along suitcases on wheels – are amazing. And Persons don't even use magic to make them. "Where are you flying to?" I asked.

"Oh, just a little tropical island, that's all," boasted Piers. "I hope you don't get *too* bored stuck here in Merrymeet, while I'm enjoying a whole week of sand, sea and sun."

"I'm sure I'll survive," I said, trying to keep a smile on my face. Everyone in Merrymeet seemed to be going somewhere for half term. My best friend Esme had gone to stay with her dad, who is separated from her mum, and lives in a big town over a hundred miles away. He had promised to take her to a theme park. And my good friends the twins had gone to see their grandma in Scotland. It looked like I might get a bit lonely. But I wasn't going to show Piers that I cared.

"I'm looking forward to staying here and enjoying the peace and quiet," I told him with a shrug, trying desperately not to let him see how jealous I felt inside.

Piers and I used to be worst enemies until I helped him out of a tricky spot with a little magic at Halloween. Even though he knows my secret, he's still a terrible show-off, but we manage to be good friends despite his boasting.

"Just don't get into any magic mischief while I'm gone." He grinned.

"I won't!" I said. But as I spoke, my fingers brushed the feathers on my special fluffy pink flamingo pen, which was hidden in my pocket. It may look like a pen but, really, it's a magic wand.

Before either of us could say another word, Piers's parents came down the steps behind him. Mrs Seymour was pulling two matching gold suitcases, each one big enough to hide a fully grown ogre inside – they looked just about as heavy as an ogre too. Mr Seymour only had one giant gold suitcase, but he also had another roll-along bag full of funny-looking metal sticks.

"Might get a game if I'm lucky," he chuckled, patting the bag of sticks as he loaded them into the car.

"Right!" I said, although I didn't have

any idea what he was talking about. I must have looked confused, because Piers grinned with delight.

"They're golf clubs, silly," he whispered.

"Ah! *Golf clubs*," I said, still none the wiser. The Person World can be such a mystery sometimes.

"Have a nice half term, Bella. I hope you're doing something fun too," said Mrs Seymour.

"I think we're just going to stay here," I said with a little sigh. My foster parents, Aunty Rose and Uncle Martin, didn't seem to have any plans. They certainly couldn't afford a deluxe desert-island holiday like the Seymours.

I tried to smile as I felt another little wave of loneliness wash over me. It really did seem as if my entire class at Merrymeet Primary were all off on some sort of adventure while I was staying here alone.

"See you in a week!" gloated Piers, waving out of the window as their big shiny car slipped out through the electric gates and sped away.

"See you when you get back," I called after him.

After all, I'd still be right here in Merrymeet. I wasn't going anywhere.

Chapter Two

I was feeling rather left behind – and a little sorry for myself too – after I watched Piers drive off to the airport. So I wandered round to our back garden to see if I could find my little kitten, Rascal. At least he wasn't going on holiday anywhere either.

I spotted the tip of his grey tail as he stalked through the long grass.

"Hello! What are you up to?" I purred

at him in Cat Chat, crouching down on my hands and knees. I can speak lots of animal languages quite fluently, like

rat, frog, and owl.
bat, toad,

In fact, I can talk to pretty much all the creatures I used to find in the Magic Realm, from tiny spiders to fierce wolves.

Cat is my favourite language, though. It's so wonderful to be able to miaow and purr with Rascal and really know what he is saying back.

"Oh, hello, Bella!" He peered at me through the grass. "Have you come to help me chase birds?"

"No, I have not!" I hissed in my sternest-sounding voice as he pounced towards a tiny robin on the path. "You know I hate it when you bully little birds like that."

Rascal twitched his whiskers. He's a pretty hopeless hunter anyway. He had missed the robin by miles and it was twittering happily with laughter at him from the edge of the birdbath.

"Well done, Mr Robin," I said, chirping to the little

red-breasted bird in his own language – or at least what I hoped might be something close to it. I have only started learning garden-bird languages since I arrived in Merrymeet. Other than owls, the only birds in the Magic Realm were cruel, sharp-beaked rooks or crows and the occasional vulture. Never anything as merry as the little robin.

"Cheerio!" he tweeted, fluttering away to a higher branch well out of Rascal's reach.

"Humph!" Rascal stuck his little grey nose in the air. "Spoilsport," he said, turning his back on me.

I didn't want to have an argument, not when he was just about the only friend I had left in Merrymeet, but I couldn't let him chase birds either, especially not as I spotted Uncle Martin coming out of the back door of our cottage.

Uncle Martin is barmy about birds. He loves watching them through his binoculars (which are another wonderful Person invention – a special pair of magic glasses to make things bigger.) He's so kind – he's always filling the bird table with fresh treats and making new nest boxes for the garden. He gets very cross when he sees Rascal up to his naughty tricks.

"Hello there, trouble!" he said as Rascal bounded over and rubbed his grey head against Uncle Martin's ankles as if the thought of chasing a little bird had never even crossed his mind.

"Ha! You're not fooling anyone!" I whispered under my breath in Cat Chat. Uncle Martin is quite used to hearing me make strange sounds with Rascal. He thinks I'm only playing, of course. He doesn't know I am having a real conversation with a cat.

"Do you want to give me a hand, Bella?" he asked, pointing to what looked like a little wooden house under his arm. "I'm just going to give this new nesting box a coat of paint so the birds can use it."

"Of course," I said, following him towards the garden shed.

Rascal licked his lips. "Yum! Bird in a box! It's just like that takeaway food you sometimes get!"

"Don't be horrid!" I hissed, running to catch up with Uncle Martin, who was striding ahead of us like a giant.

"This one is actually a special sort of nesting box," he explained. "For owls!"

"Fluttering feathers!" I cried excitedly. "Do you really think an owl might come and live in our garden?"

"I don't see why not. That's what this

nest box is all about," he said, laying it down on the bench inside his shed. "If we give it a nice coat of paint to protect the wood, then nail it up in a tree, it should make an ideal nesting site."

"That would be amazing. I love owls." I grinned. "They're so cute."

"What's so great about owls? Big-eyed balls of feather!" huffed Rascal, stalking away with his tail in the air.

"Come back!" I purred. "They're not as cute as you, of course..." But it was no good. He was halfway up the garden path already. Kittens are very jealous!

"Right," said Uncle Martin. "What colour house do you think an owl would like?" He pulled out a box of old paint tins from under the bench.

"Maybe yellow," I said, spotting a tin left over from when Uncle Martin had painted our own front door. "Or blue." Like my bedroom. "Or green." That one was from the garden gate. "There are so many to choose from."

"I tell you what," Uncle Martin chuckled, "you have a think about it and paint it when you've chosen. I'll nip back up to the house and fetch my long ladder, then we'll be ready to put it up in the tree as soon as we're done."

"All right!" I agreed, picking up a paintbrush. "I'll make up my mind and get started."

In the end, I decided to go with rainbow stripes! There were so many lovely colours, I couldn't pick just one.

By the time I'd finished the bright green stripe, halfway up the box, I was surprised that Uncle Martin wasn't back. I looked up and saw he was still inside the house, talking to Aunty Rose by the kitchen window. From the way they kept nodding their heads and even waving their arms as they spoke, it seemed they must be discussing something important. They kept glancing in my direction too. I waved, but they didn't see me.

I wondered what it could all be about.

"Grown-ups!" I muttered under my breath. "Who knows?" And I got on with painting the last few stripes on the birdhouse, pushing thoughts of anything else out of my head. When I was finished, the little owl house really did look splendid and bright. I wiped my hands on an old rag and was standing back to admire my handiwork when I had a brilliant, *magical* idea.

I dug my hand into my pocket and pulled out my wand.

My mean aunt Hemlock had warned me never to do *any* magic *ever again*, once she'd banished me to the Person World . . . and for once she was right about something. Casting hexes and muttering incantations just isn't normal around here. Persons do not take kindly to the idea of being turned into frogs – and who can blame them? One little wave of my wand could ruin everything. I dread to think how Aunty Rose and Uncle Martin would feel if they knew they had fostered a young witch. But sometimes, I can't help myself. The magic seems to bubble up inside me and I can't resist a teeny-tiny spell. Only if I think it will make things better, of course – never to do any horrid witchy harm.

That feeling was fizzing inside me now as I looked at the little owl box.

I poked my head around the door of the shed and saw that Uncle Martin and Aunty Rose both had their backs to the kitchen window, so they couldn't see what I was doing.

Quick as a flash, I waved my fluffy pink pen in the air three times above the freshly painted nest box as I muttered a tiny little spell.

Bless this box so it will make
The perfect house for an owl to take!

A shower of golden stars shot out the end of my wand and hovered over the little nest box for a moment.

"Perfect!"

I whispered. I know how exciting it is to have a lovely new home – I'd never felt as happy anywhere as I did at Honeysuckle Cottage. Now an owl would have the chance to feel like that, too. The box would be safe and dry – it was bright and cheerful – and protected with a little magic as well.

"Leaping lizards!" I nearly jumped out of my skin as Uncle Martin appeared in the doorway behind me. "You have been busy," he said. "Rainbow stripes and gold stars too."

"Stars?" I said, stuffing my flamingo pen into my pocket and staring at the owl box. Uncle Martin was right. As well as the brightly coloured stripes, there were glittering stars sprinkled on the roof as well. It was as if a shimmer of the magic I made had been caught in the wet paint.

"Well, I think it looks jolly smart," said

Uncle Martin, leaning his long ladder against the side of the shed. "I didn't even know we had any gold paint to make stars with … but I'm sure the owls will be delighted."

"I hope so!" I gulped, pleased that he didn't seem to be going to ask too many questions.

"Come on! Let's leave it to dry for a bit. Then we can hang it in the tall oak tree. That should make a good nesting spot," he said.

"Perfect!" I agreed.

"And meanwhile, we can have a cup of tea. Aunty Rose has just put the kettle on," he said.

I was about to ask what they had been talking about earlier, when Aunty Rose poked her head out of the window. She had her usual happy grin on her round apple cheeks.

"Tea's ready," she called. "And I've just baked a fresh chocolate cake if anyone would like to try a slice?"

"Yum!" I cried, dashing across the lawn. I think Aunty Rose is probably the best baker in the whole of the Person World.

"I know chocolate cake is your favourite, Bella." She grinned as I skidded through the kitchen door. "And it is half term, after all!" Her eyes were sparkling with delight – she really does spoil me rotten.

"Bella definitely deserves an extra-big piece," Uncle Martin agreed, as he pulled

up a chair beside me. "She has painted the smartest rainbow owl box I have ever seen."

"Thank you!" I said as he cut me an enormous oozy slice. He spoils me rotten too!

"Delicious!" I said, taking a big gooey bite. I didn't need a fancy trip to a tropical island to have a good time, after all. I could have plenty of fun right here in Merrymeet with Uncle Martin and Aunty Rose.

"Do you think an owl might come and nest in the box before half term is over?" I asked, through a second sticky mouthful of cake.

"Maybe," said Uncle Martin. "You'll just have to listen out for a hoot when it gets dark this evening."

"I will!" I said excitedly. "Maybe I'll stay up all night, and wait for an owl to come."

"Not tonight," said Aunty Rose firmly. "We've got a big day tomorrow."

"A big day?" I asked. "What do you mean?"

My heart was suddenly pounding. I don't like surprises. Whenever anything unexpected happened in the Magic Realm it was always bad! Like the time Aunt Hemlock promised she wasn't going to turn me into a slug for three whole weeks ... so she turned me a maggot instead.

But Uncle Martin and Aunty Rose just shook their heads.

"You'll have to wait and see," they said.

Chapter Three

"Twit-woo! Twit-woo! If there's an owl out there, please come." I had been sitting on my bedroom window sill calling out in Owl language across the dark garden for what seemed like hours. Uncle Martin had hung the little rainbow-painted box in the very top of the old oak tree, and I could just see the magic stars twinkling in the darkness.

"Come along, owls. We've made you a

home," I hooted softly. But there was still no reply.

I had tried my best to get to sleep, but I just couldn't. I was too busy wondering what the big secret about tomorrow morning might be. Aunty Rose and Uncle Martin had been acting very strangely all day, whispering and nudging each other when they thought I wasn't looking – and Uncle Martin kept poking about in the cupboard under the stairs.

I told myself there was probably a perfectly normal explanation, but I was starting to feel a little bit worried.

"Twit-woo! Twit-woo!" I called again.

"Shh!" hissed Rascal, who was curled up in a ball on my bed. "Some of us are trying to get some sleep."

"Sorry!" I whispered, climbing into bed myself and snuggling down beside him. "I'll give up now, I promise."

Rascal had a point. It was very late. Aunty Rose and Uncle Martin had probably gone to sleep hours ago. "But I really do wish an owl would come and nest in our garden," I whispered. "Uncle Martin would be so excited."

"Never trust an owl." Rascal yawned. "They've got big eyes and they're always blinking. . ."

"What's wrong with that? You've got big eyes and you're always blinking too," I said with a yawn of my own. "But you don't need to worry, Rascal. There can't be any owls for miles around. Otherwise they would have surely heard me calling and come. Don't you think?"

Rascal didn't answer. I could hear him snoring gently like a baby troll.

"Goodnight," I whispered. "See you in the mor. . ." But I must have fallen asleep too, because the next thing I knew, Aunty Rose was standing above my bed, gently shaking me awake.

"Come on, Bella, sweetie. It's time to get up."

"Get up?" I murmured. "Am I late for school?"

"No!" Aunty Rose laughed. "It's half term, remember," she said, helping me into a pair of jeans and a thick jumper.

As I stumbled sleepily downstairs, Uncle Martin was standing in the hallway with the front door open behind him. It was still dark outside.

"Where are we going?" I said. "And what in the name of Merlin's beard is all that stuff?!"

There were bags and blankets and boxes all over the hall. I could see a fold-up garden chair poking out from under a big pack of toilet rolls and there were piles of

clothes everywhere. I even glimpsed a giant-sized tin of baked beans and a frying pan.

"Wait!" I said, suddenly wide awake. "We're not leaving home are we? For ever, I mean?" There seemed to be enough provisions here to last a year. "I don't want to leave Honeysuckle Cottage." Perhaps it was the shock of going to bed so late and being woken up so early, but my heart was pounding and my eyes were suddenly full of tears. "I love it here. It's our home."

"Of course it's home!" Aunty Rose put her arm around my shoulders. "Honeysuckle Cottage will always be your home, Bella. Uncle Martin and I promise you will never have to leave unless you want to."

"And a promise is a serious thing," said

Uncle Martin gravely.

"It certainly is," agreed Aunty Rose. "A real promise can never be broken lightly."

"Not like a china plate?" I said, smiling a little again.

"Not at all like a china plate," agreed Aunty Rose. "Or the glass in a window – a promise is far stronger than that."

"Stronger even than an iron bar," said Uncle Martin putting on a funny deep voice. "Or the bricks that make Honeysuckle Cottage into such a lovely strong safe home."

"Thank you!" I said with a great gush of breath. I knew they really meant it. My home was here with them – at Honeysuckle Cottage – for as long as I wanted it to be.

"But we did think you might like to go away for a bit," said Uncle Martin gently. "Not for ever… Just for a week."

"On holiday," said Aunty Rose.

"Holiday? You mean now? For half term?" I cried, remembering how much I had been longing for a trip.

"We saw how lonely you were with no friends around," explained Aunty Rose. "So we came up with a last-minute expedition of our own."

"Really? A holiday?" My mouth dropped open in surprise. Then I clapped my hands in sheer delight and leapt into the air with a wild star jump.

"Bursting butterflies, this is the best surprise ever. Where are we going to go?" I asked. I knew we couldn't afford to fly off to a fancy tropical island like Piers and his family – but that didn't matter one little bit. I had never been on a holiday anywhere in my entire life, so it would all be a wonderful new adventure no matter where we went.

"Camping, of course!" Uncle Martin beamed. "It's the best sort of holiday there is!"

"I can see why you thought we might be leaving for ever," said Aunty Rose. "Your uncle Martin does like to pack just about everything we own. He'd bring the kitchen sink, if he could."

"Oh, I'll get it if you like," I cried in a huge rush of excitement. "With magic!" It would be quite an easy spell to lift the sink up out of the draining board and add it to the pile of camping supplies in the hall. But as soon as the words were out, I put my hand over my mouth in shock as I realized I had actually said them out loud. "Er... I mean ... I *could* get it if I was able to do spells. Which I can't ... obviously." I blushed furiously, horrified I had almost given my secret away.

But Uncle Martin just laughed. "Ha! I

might need a spell or two to help put the tent up later."

Luckily, Persons always seem to think I'm joking when I mention magic by mistake. But, as I pulled on my coat, I slipped my hand deep inside the pocket and felt the soft feathers of my pink flamingo wand. I smiled, wondering if I might be able to magically help Uncle Martin with the tent later after all.

"Ready, then?" said Aunty Rose.

"Ready," I agreed.

"Let's get the car loaded," said Uncle Martin with a grin.

I was just about to pick up the giant can of baked beans, when I heard a miaow on the stairs behind me.

"I hope you've got some cat food too?" purred Rascal.

I stopped dead in my tracks. In my

34

excitement and surprise, I had forgotten all about the little kitten.

"Aunty Rose?" I said slowly. "Do cats come on camping trips?"

"I'm sorry, poppet. I'm afraid not." She shook her head.

"Oh no!" I stretched out my hand towards Rascal.

But he arched his back and spat at me from the top of the stairs.

I thought my heart would break as he stalked away with his tail in the air.

It was just getting light as we pulled out of the driveway and our little red car spluttered under the weight of everything Uncle Martin had packed.

35

I might be fluent in Cat Chat, but I never knew until that moment I could lip-read too.

Rascal's face was pressed up against the window in the front room.

"Traitor!" he mouthed.

"Stop!" I cried and Uncle Martin slammed on the brakes.

"What's the matter?" he asked.

"Please," I begged for the hundredth time. "Can't Rascal come?"

"I'm sorry." Aunty Rose leant over from the front seat and put her hand on my knee. "He might get lost at the campsite. But don't worry, he won't be shut in the house for long. Mrs Brimblecombe from the post office has promised to come and let him out as soon as she's had her breakfast. She'll check up on him regularly and feed him too."

"Five meals a day, plus second helpings, if

I know Mrs Brimblecombe." Uncle Martin laughed. "I wouldn't be surprised if our little Rascal is as fat as her budgie, Billy, by the time we get home. I expect he'll want to go and live in the post office by then!" he said as the car moved off again.

"Oh, don't say that!" I turned in my seat to wave one last time, but Rascal had disappeared.

He was probably sulking under the sofa. Or perhaps he'd gone upstairs to leave a furball on the end of my bed to punish me for leaving him behind.

"Don't worry, you'll be well looked after and we'll be back soon," I promised, calling out of the car window as we drove away. After all, Uncle Martin and Aunty Rose were right. We were only going on a little holiday. I would be home long before Rascal could miss me too much.

Chapter Four

No sooner had our car left Merrymeet than it started to pour with rain.

The windscreen wipers whooshed back and forth, back and forth, like a young witch practising wand work.

"Never mind," said Uncle Martin brightly. "A spot of rain won't spoil our camping trip."

"A spot?" I said, peering through the steamed-up car window. I hadn't seen a downpour like this since I lived in the Magic Realm. It always rains there. Every day. If it isn't drizzling, it's pouring. And if it isn't pouring, it's bucketing down with hail.

"I'm sure it'll brighten up soon," said Aunty Rose hopefully, as we drove along water-logged country lanes. "I think I can see a sliver of blue sky." But the rain kept on falling as we splashed through damp villages and sloshed up and down slippery roads, over soggy cloud-covered hills until we reached the campsite at last.

"Oh dear," said Uncle Martin, as we slid to a stop outside a wooden gate which was firmly closed. "It doesn't look like we're going to be camping here after all."

I squinted through the window and read a dripping-wet notice pinned to the gate:

The campsite was so soggy it looked more like a lake than a grassy field. There was no sign of anybody else for miles around.

"Look! There's some big woods over there," said Aunty Rose, pointing through the rain. Maybe we could pitch our tent under the trees. It would keep us nice and dry."

"Good idea," said Uncle Martin and he

turned the car down a windy lane which led through the forest. "We'll see if there's a house down here and ask if it's all right to camp. I wouldn't want to just trespass on somebody else's land."

"Righty-ho!" agreed Aunty Rose cheerily.

That's the wonderful thing about my foster parents. Uncle Martin and Aunty Rose always stay cheerful, no matter what happens. A little bit of rain wasn't going to dampen their spirits – or ruin our camping trip.

"Hooray!" I cheered, catching the brightness of their mood too. "It'll be a real adventure to camp in the woods."

But the lane we were following turned out not to be a proper road at all. It was more like a cart track really. And before long we were wheel-deep in thick, oozy mud.

"Gracious," giggled Aunty Rose, peeping out of her window. "This stuff's stickier than my chocolate icing!"

"I think we'd better go back," said Uncle Martin, and he changed gear. The car made a noise like a roaring dragon, but it didn't move. It wouldn't go backwards ... and, as Uncle Martin shifted the gears again, we realized it wouldn't go forwards any more either.

"We're stuck!" said Uncle Martin simply.

I didn't dare risk a spell to help out – not with my foster parents sitting right in front of me in the car. They'd be sure to notice if I suddenly whipped out my flamingo wand and got rid of all the mud.

"You better phone the breakdown service, Rose." Uncle Martin sighed. "See if someone can come and give us a tow."

"Oh dear!" Aunty Rose's pink-apple cheeks flushed red as she rummaged through her handbag. "I don't think I have my phone with me. I do have a tin-opener though," she said, holding that up in the air as if it was a magic golden key which could solve all our problems. "I was worried I'd left that behind."

"But no phone?" I asked, feeling a little nervous as I glanced out at the dark, looming trees all around us. I had never been in a forest in the Person World before. All I know is that in the Magic Realm, a shadowy wood like this one would be full of spooks and spectres and ghouls just waiting for unsuspecting travellers to come by.

"I must have left my phone sitting on the kitchen counter by the kettle," Aunty Rose groaned. "I was about to pack it when I remembered we needed teabags. I think I may got a bit distracted by packing those instead."

"Hmm," said Uncle Martin, rummaging

through his pockets and finding his own phone. "I'm not sure it would have made any difference anyway." He scowled at the screen (which was crackled all over like a spider web from where he had dropped it out of tree while birdwatching). He tapped it several times and then shook it and held the handset out of the car window. "There's no reception here at all."

"We really are in the wild, aren't we?" I said, peering out of the window as Uncle Martin turned off the engine and gave up trying to shift the bogged-down car.

"Never mind! It's half the fun, feeling cut off from the rest of the world when you're on a camping trip. It means there'll be lots of birds to see," he said, swivelling round in his seat with an excited smile. "And look, it's stopped raining, at last." He pointed through the back window.

"So it has," agreed Aunty Rose, turning round in her seat too. "I think the sun's coming out."

They were right. As we climbed carefully out of the car, trying not to sink up to our knees in mud, I could see a tiny snake-thin patch of blue sky through the trees.

"Look! There's a little clearing through there," said Uncle Martin, setting off down a twisty path between the tall, dark tree trunks.

I followed, and sure enough, a moment later, we stepped out into a pretty woodland glade, ringed with wild flowers.

"Fluttering fairies, it's perfect!" I cried and all my fear of the dark woods vanished in an instant.

"Oh, isn't it lovely?" cooed Aunty Rose, catching up with us as she hurried along the path carrying an old tin kettle and a box of teabags.

"It is the prettiest place I have ever seen," I whispered under my breath as a shiver of excitement tingled inside me. It was the sort of woodland glade where pixies might come to dance or wood nymphs would doze.

As the last drops of drying rain caught the sun, a shimmering arch appeared above our heads.

"A rainbow," laughed Aunty Rose. "It's just like your owl box."

"This is going to be the best holiday ever!" I said.

Chapter Five

I have never EVER been more desperate to use magic than when I was helping Uncle Martin to put up the tent.

"We'd better set up camp while it is still dry and light," he said as Aunty Rose started brewing tea on the clever little fold-out stove she had brought along. "There's not much else we can do tonight. Tomorrow I'll go and look for a farm to see if they can telephone for help with the car."

It sounded like a good plan. But I had no idea the silky, billowing blue tent would have a life all of its own. It was like wrestling a demon. No sooner was one side up than the other fell down. At one point the whole thing collapsed on my head – I wouldn't have minded too much, but it had a funny damp smell inside, like musty goblin socks.

Uncle Martin kept waving the tent pegs around like a dragon-slaying knight.

"Got you, you brute!" he bellowed … then realized the whole thing was inside out. His long legs got tied up in the ropes somehow, and he fell over backwards in a tent-smothered heap.

"Nearly got it!" he said, brightly.

My fingers were itching to pull out my flamingo wand and help. With one *swoosh* through the air, the job could have been done in a second, but I couldn't risk Uncle Martin or Aunty Rose seeing me. So instead, it was another whole hour before the wobbly little shelter was standing up by itself.

It was already starting to get dark by the time we were finished.

"Sparkling starfish!" I cried as a string of fairy lights Uncle Martin had hung in the trees suddenly twinkled into life. If I hadn't known better, I'd have thought he was a wizard who had used magic to light them. There was definitely no electricity out here in the middle of the forest.

Uncle Martin smiled as I stared in amazement. "They're powered by sunlight," he explained. "Marvellous, isn't it? They store up solar power all day long to use as electricity when it gets dark."

"Brilliant!" I agreed. I'd thought Piers's roll-along suitcase was clever, but this was an even more ingenious invention and not a whiff of magic involved.

"I've packed some windup torches too," said Uncle Martin proudly, holding a little green one shaped like a funny frog. "All you do is give its legs a squeeze like this..." He began to pump them up and down. "And the light comes on – see?"

"Shimmering salamanders, that's fantastic!" I gasped.

"I brought it for you," said Uncle Martin. "You might need it when it gets really dark."

"Thank you," I said, shining the torch at the shadowy trees and watching the light dance over the branches like a yellow ghost. As I was playing, a delicious smell wafted towards me.

"Yum!" The woodland glade was full of

the wonderful whiff of sizzling sausages.

"Ready!" called Aunty Rose.

"Scrumptious!" said Uncle Martin as he ladled baked beans on to our tin plates. "Food always tastes better in the open air,"

"Especially if you've worked hard for it," agreed Aunty Rose.

It was true. I was absolutely starving – and although it had taken ages to set up camp, it had been fun too. The woodland glade looked very homely now in the flickering glow of the fairy lanterns with the cheerful tent in the middle like a little house with three fold-out chairs and a picnic table beside it.

But no sooner had I sat on one of the wobbly chairs and lifted my fork to my mouth, than it began to pour with rain again.

It didn't really matter though. We all

screamed with laughter, darted inside the tent and ate our supper there, listening to the *plip-plop* of rain splashing against the rustling blue fabric above our heads.

"Skidding squids, it really is waterproof!" I said, impressed by the little tent at last. Aunt Hemlock's cave was never as dry as this. Every day, when it rained in the Magic Realm, great drips came pouring down through the roof.

When we'd finished eating we washed up – which was easy as the bowl we'd left outside was already full of rainwater. Then we played cards by torchlight and settled down for bed. It was a perfect evening.

"You can have that red sleeping bag, Bella," said Aunty Rose.

"What? We're going to sleep in bags?" I asked, amazed.

Uncle Martin laughed.

But Aunty Rose gave my hand a little squeeze. "You are funny," she said gently. I think she worries sometimes what my life must have been like before I came to live with them in Merrymeet. She thinks I grew up in the Person World, of course. But there are so many things I don't know. It must seem very strange to her when I say the wrong thing, but she never presses me to talk about it.

"You can tell our Bella's never been camping before, that's for sure," Uncle Martin chuckled in his own kind way.

As soon as I saw the sleeping bags, I realized my mistake. When I heard we'd be sleeping in bags, I'd expected something like the ones we bring the shopping home in from the supermarket, or maybe a Person-sized version of the book bag I have at school. But I was relieved to see a big soft roll

 like a squishy duvet with a zip around two sides. I felt as cosy as a glow-worm as soon as I was snuggled down inside.

"I don't think I'll ever to get sleep, though. Camping is far too exciting for that," I said as I listened to the sound of rain pattering above my head and the wind whispering in the trees. "Being in a tent is like sleeping in a little burrow underground."

"What a lovely idea," murmured Aunty Rose, tucked up in her sleeping bag beside Uncle Martin on the other side of the tent.

I thought of all the little creatures that must be out there in the woods, snuggling down for the night too: rabbits and tiny mice in their warm, dry homes beneath the earth, and squirrels nesting high in the trees. Meanwhile, foxes and badgers would be just waking up, ready to explore the woods at night.

"And owls too," I said with a yawn.

"What that's about owls?" asked Uncle Martin. He sounded just as sleepy as I felt. I'm not sure I even answered him before I drifted off into a deep sleep as if the floor of the forest glade beneath us were a soft feather bed.

"Twit-woo! Twit-woo!"

An owl was calling.

At first, I thought it was a dream ... perhaps because I'd gone to sleep thinking about owls. Then I realized I was awake. I thought the owl must be calling out from the new nest box we'd put up in the oak tree at Honeysuckle Cottage. It was only as I sat up and blinked that I remembered where I was. I wasn't at home in Merrymeet at all. We were camping in the forest.

I could hear Aunty Rose and Uncle Martin snoring in time with each other in their sleeping bags at the opposite end of the tent. Uncle Martin's snore was deep and rumbly like a dozing giant. Aunty Rose's was softer but just as steady, like a jolly elf sleeping off a good meal.

Good job Rascal isn't here, I thought. *He snores louder than both of them.* I smiled to myself and hugged my knees as I sat up in my sleeping bag, listening out for the owl.

But when the hoot echoed through the woods again, it sounded shrill and frightened. "Twit-woooo! Twit-woooo!"

Something was wrong.

"Twit-woo!" shrieked the frightened-sounding voice. "Help me, please!"

I slipped out of my sleeping bag and crept to the flap at the front of the tent. I unzipped it as quietly as I could so as not to wake my sleeping foster parents, and peeped out.

The rain had stopped at long last. The fairy lights were still twinkling, and a bright moon was shining through the trees so that the little forest glade seemed as if it had been painted silver.

I was just thinking how pretty it looked – as if it had been enchanted by woodland sprites - when the owl screeched again.

"Twit-woo! Twit-woo!" From the sound of the frightened hoot, it seemed like the owl was a girl – and very young too. "Help me! Help me if you can."

A tiny speckled bird came hurtling through the moonlit trees towards me.

"Stop!" I called softly to her in owl hoot. "What is it? What's wrong?"

I scrambled out of the tent, quickly zipping the flaps tightly shut behind me.

There was no answer. I blinked and looked all around the moonlit glade, but the owl had vanished.

Chapter Six

I peered into the dark trees at the edge of our woodland campsite, turning in circles as I searched for the tiny speckle-feathered owlet. Perhaps the little creature had already flown away – but why was she crying out like that? Her trembling hoots had sounded so afraid.

Now I was safely outside the tent, I called out again more loudly. "Twit-woo! Twit-woo! Are you there, little owl?"

Suddenly I spotted a pale shimmer of feathers. She was perched among the pretty fairy lights, gently lit by their warm glow. I could see that she was trembling.

"Hello. I'm Bella." I took a step closer and held out my arm, hoping she would swoop down and land on it. But she just hopped nervously away along the string of lights. "What's your name?" I coaxed.

"I'm Little Woo," she hooted softly. "And I'm lost."

"Oh dear," I said, as she hopped anxiously from foot to foot. "Where are you trying to get to, Little Woo?"

"Home to my family," she said. Her round feathery face was flooded with moonlight. I had never seen any creature look so sad.

"I was out flying, but I've lost my way, and I don't like being in the forest alone at night because ... because... Oh, dear. You'll laugh at me," she hooted. Then she blinked and hid her head under her wing.

"I won't laugh. I promise," I said, tiptoeing a little closer across the damp grass in my bare feet. "Tell me why you don't like being in the forest, Little Woo."

"It's ... because ... because ... *I-am-scared-of-the-dark*," she said in a great rush.

"Scared of the dark? Oh you poor thing." My lips twitched – not because I was going to giggle, but because I wanted to smile encouragingly. I know just how it feels to be frightened of something, and the poor little thing looked so sad.

"See!" she squawked and buried her head again. "You're laughing at me. I knew you would."

"No, I'm not. Honestly! I'll tell you a secret, Little Woo. I'm scared of the dark sometimes too," I said, rubbing my arms to try and keep warm. I was only wearing my blue spotty pyjamas and the spring night air was chilly.

"It's all right for you," she mumbled through her feathers. "You're a girl. I'm an owl. Owls aren't supposed to be scared of the dark."

"Nonsense," I said encouragingly. "Anyone would be scared in this gloomy old forest."

"Do you really think so?" Little Woo peeped out at me from under her wing.

"I know so," I said, glancing at the dark, menacing trees all around us. They really did look pretty spooky beyond the twinkling safety of the glade. "I know golden eagles who'd melt like butter if you asked them to fly in there. And vampire bats who'd vanish faster than the wind if you even suggested it."

Little Woo blinked. "But that still doesn't help me," she said. "I'll have to fly back in amongst the dark trees if I ever want to find my family again."

"Yes," I said slowly, "I suppose that's true."

"Please, Bella. Will you come with me?" said Little Woo. She flew down and hopped along the back of a picnic chair right beside me. "Please help me find my family." She was staring at me imploringly with her big golden-yellow eyes. "It won't take long. We must be somewhere quite nearby. I'm sure I remember flying over this clearing with my parents on our way home once before."

I glanced towards the warm tent, then towards the dark, scary trees, and then at the safe, warm tent again. I knew the sensible thing to do was to get back into my cosy sleeping bag, pull it up over my head and leave the little owl to cope by herself. But one look at her big sad eyes and I knew I couldn't do it. Suppose Rascal was lost in a deep dark forest like this one – I'd want somebody to help him, that's for sure.

"All right!" I said firmly. "I'll come."

"Oh, thank you, Bella. Twit-woo. Twit-woo." Little Woo hopped right up on to my shoulder and shyly nibbled my ear. "Thank you so much."

"You're welcome!" I giggled. "But wait one minute. If I'm going to come with you, I'll need to grab a coat and some shoes. I can't go into the forest with bare feet." I stretched out my hand and very gently touched Little Woo's soft downy feathers. She felt so snug, she might as well have been wrapped in a warm duvet, but I was already shivering from the damp grass and chilly night air.

"Please hurry! My family will be so worried," she said, fluttering back to the safe glow of the fairy lights to wait.

"One minute!" I promised, and I ducked back into the tent.

Uncle Martin and Aunty Rose were still snoring merrily. For a moment, I thought about waking them up to tell them where I was going. But they were sleeping so deeply ... and, anyway, how would I explain to them that a baby owl, who was afraid of the dark, had spoken to me and told me she was lost? They'd think I'd gone mad.

Little Woo was sure it wouldn't take long. *And I won't go far into the forest*, I promised myself as I pulled on a pair of warm woolly socks and wriggled into my thick coat. I slipped my hands into both pockets and felt my wand buried deep in one and the funny little frog torch in the other. Knowing they were there made me feel braver already.

"I'll stick to the edge of the clearing and be back in no time," I whispered out loud, as if telling Aunty Rose and Uncle Martin what I was up to after all. But they just kept snoring.

"Twit-woo! Twit-woo," hooted Little Woo impatiently.

I pulled on my yellow wellies, which were just inside the door of the tent, and was about to slip out when I had a terrible thought. What if Uncle Martin and Aunty Rose woke up and found my sleeping bag empty? They'd be worried sick when they couldn't find me – just like poor Little Woo's family who thought she was lost now.

I took my wand from my pocket and waved it over their sleeping heads.

If you wake and I am gone,
Just keep calm and carry on!
Don't even notice I'm not here,
Until I'm back and reappear.

A shimmering shower of magic fell gently on their snoring heads like dream dust.

Now if they woke, they wouldn't be anxious about where I had got to – they would just potter happily about the campsite until I returned. I ducked out of the tent and stepped towards the dark, twisted trees.

"Come on, Little Woo," I said as she fluttered down and landed on my shoulder. "Let's take you home."

Chapter Seven

I glanced back at the tent one last time as Little Woo perched on my shoulder.

"Ready?" I asked and I stepped into the edge of the dark trees.

"Promise you won't leave me," she said.

"I promise," I agreed. I remembered what Aunty Rose and Uncle Martin had said about what a strong and powerful thing a promise was. I would have to keep my pledge to Little Woo now I had made it.

"Do you promise you'll take me all the way home?" she said.

"Yes!" I answered solemnly. "I promise I'll take you back to your family. I give you my word."

At least Aunty Rose and Uncle Martin wouldn't worry if they found me gone. Not now I'd put a spell on them. And I was sure I would be back before first light. Little Woo had said it wasn't far.

"Thank you!" she hooted in a tiny voice so quiet I could barely hear her. I felt her sharp claws digging into my shoulder as we walked deeper into the dark forest. The light of the full moon was hidden now and I reached into my pocket for the torch.

"There," hooted Little Woo as the light fell on the snowy-white trunk of a silver birch tree. "It's just past here, then there's a thin, twisted pine and... Oh, dear. Maybe just a little further still."

On we went, deeper into the dark wood.

"Oh, yes!" hooted Little Woo, from time to time, and she flapped her wings with excitement. "We're getting closer. I am sure I remember that tall tree ... and that short one ... and that funny, twisted one which looks an old woman bent over a cauldron."

"Glimmering goblins!" I shuddered. "Don't say things like that."

Little Woo was right, the funny old tree did look just like a witch bending over a spell. Yet when I glanced back over my shoulder again, the shadows must have shifted – I couldn't see the funny misshapen tree at all. It was as if it had got up and walked away. But that couldn't be true. Could it? Trees couldn't walk. Not here in the Person World.

But my heart was still pounding as we stumbled onwards. I began to worry if we'd ever find Little Woo's nest site in the vast woods. The thick, dark trees grew closer and closer together, so that I often had to squeeze between their rough woody trunks to move forward at all.

"Little Woo?" I whispered. "Are you sure it's this way? You said it wasn't far. And we've been walking for ages now."

I stopped and looked over my shoulder.

"You can't turn back." Little Woo flapped her wings desperately. "I promised I'd bring you to her."

"I know," I agreed. For a moment I thought the little owl was still talking about the promise I had made to take her home. It was only as I took another step forward that I realized what she had actually said. *She* had promised to bring *me* to someone.

My throat tightened and I swallowed hard before I spoke again. "Little Woo?" I asked, trying to keep my voice steady. "What are you talking about?" Perhaps I had heard her wrong after all. "Did you promise to bring *me* to someone?"

"No," said Little Woo. But her hoot was so high-pitched and nervous she sounded more like a screeching seagull than an owl. "No, no, Belladonna Broomstick!"

"*Belladonna Broomstick*?" I whispered and my heart leapt in my chest. "How do you know my full name? I never told it to you, Little Woo. I just said that I was called Bella." Nobody in the whole of the Person World calls me Belladonna – it was the very first thing I changed on the day that I arrived in Merrymeet.

The owl was silent.

"Little Woo," I said desperately. "Little

Woo? You have to tell me what's going on." I twisted my neck to try and glance round at her on my shoulder. In the same moment, my feet slipped from underneath me on the wet forest floor.

"I'm sorry, Bella. So sorry!" I heard Little Woo's wings flap past my ear as she took off into the air and I tumbled over and over, rolling down a steep bank between the trees.

"Sorry?" I gasped, trying to stop myself from tumbling. "Sorry about what, Little Woo?"

But before the owl could answer I reached the bottom of the slope and felt my body hit something cold and wet. It was a feeling I knew only too well – like being slapped in the face with a cold, dead fish.

"No!" I cried. But I knew it was already too late.

I had passed right through the Curtain

of Invisibility and out on to the other side. I was back in the Magic Realm again.

When I stopped rolling at last, I saw Little Woo circling above my head in the strange green moonlight.

"You tricked me!" I gasped, staggering to my feet. "You said you needed my help. But you didn't, did you? This was your plan all along ... to bring me here?"

"I really am so sorry," she said, with a forlorn hoot.

"Why?" I asked, my stomach flipping over like a pancake. "Why would you do that?" I couldn't believe that Little Woo, who looked so soft and sweet and fluffy, had done such a terrible thing. She had brought me to the one place I never wanted to come to ever again. She had brought me back to the Magic Realm.

I shivered with horror. The thick forest with its little glade, where I had been camping with Uncle Martin and Aunty Rose, was gone. Instead, we were on a scrubby patch of moonlit wasteland where nothing much seemed to grow at all. There were a few scraggy thorn trees and sharp rocks jutting up from the ground like broken teeth. I leapt forward, desperately hoping it was not too late and I could still find my way back to the Person World. But it was hopeless. No matter how much I waved my arms about, I couldn't feel the curtain that separated the two worlds any more. I was still so dizzy from rolling down the hill, I wasn't even sure I was feeling for it in the right direction. That's the trouble with looking for something invisible: your eyes are no use at all. You just have to grope around until you find it – and I was having no luck.

"Oh, Little Woo. What have you done?" I wailed. I had been clinging tightly to the little frog torch all this time, but I slipped it into my pocket and sighed. There was no point in shining it. Even a light as bright as the sun wouldn't help me find an invisible curtain no one can see.

I slumped down and buried my head in my hands. "Who made you do this, Little Woo?" I asked.

The only answer was a dry laugh, as a shadow blocked out the light of the moon.

That wasn't Little Woo's shadow.

I turned my head and stared up at the dark figure hunched on her broomstick like a vulture.

A shiver ran down my spine.

"Aunt Hemlock," I whispered. "It's you."

Chapter Eight

Aunt Hemlock landed her broomstick beside me.

"Well, well! Look who we have here."

I leapt to my feet but my legs were shaking and I knew it was pointless to run. I thought for a wild moment I might try magic. Yet, even though my wand was hidden in my pocket, I would never dare to use it against Aunt Hemlock in a face-to-face spell fight. She is a very powerful witch. She could turn

mc into a speck of dust to be blown away by the wind at a moment's notice.

"Welcome back!" Aunt Hemlock cackled with laughter. It was a horrible sound like fingernails scratching on a pane of glass. All I could do was take a step away and shiver as an icy breeze whistled over the lonely marshes. It was raining too, of course — almost snowing. Cold sleet dripped down the back of my neck.

"Twit-woo!" Little Woo was shivering too, perched on a nearby thorn tree.

"I suppose you want a reward, do you, you feathery fleabag?" Aunt Hemlock dug in her pocket and tossed the little owl what looked like a shrivelled lizard's tail. "There! That's for bringing Belladonna to me!"

"So I was right. You did trick me, Little Woo!" I gasped. "You were working for Aunt Hemlock all along."

Little Woo ignored the treat. She just stared up at me with her big yellow eyes.

"I'm so sorry, Bella," she hooted in a tiny voice, but I turned my head away and folded my arms.

This was all her fault. I had never been so angry with an animal in my whole life. She had lured me here with her sad story of being lost and afraid in the dark wood – all because her wicked mistress told her to.

"I've been a fungus-headed fool!" I groaned. Of course Little Woo wasn't scared. Not really. She was an owl, and who'd ever heard of an owl being scared of the dark ... even if she was only a very tiny one – not much bigger than a guinea pig really.

"Bella?" she hooted again.

But Aunt Hemlock clapped her hands.

"Get lost, you feather-brained puffball!"

she growled. "There's no more lizard tails for you. Go on. Shoo!" She bent down, picked up a sharp stone and threw it at the little owl.

"Stop!" I cried. I might be furious with Little Woo, but I couldn't bear to see her hurt. "Fly away quick," I urged and she spread her wings and swooped off over the moonlit marshes.

"Pathetic!" cackled Aunt Hemlock. "You always were soppy about animals, Belladonna. No wonder it was so simple for me to trick you into coming back."

"You knew I'd help a lost creature. Especially a young one," I mumbled, seeing clearly now how Aunt Hemlock had set her trap.

"Of course I did. I didn't need magic to get you here this time," cackled Aunt Hemlock. She was well aware that, unless

I wanted to leave the Person World for myself, even her wickedest spell was not powerful enough to force me away from my loving new home with Uncle Martin and Aunty Rose. "One hoot from that silly fluffy bird and you came tumbling back all of your own free will."

"Whimpering warlocks! I've been so stupid." I buried my head in my hands and groaned. It had been so easy for Aunt Hemlock to trick me. I had promised to bring Little Woo back to her family. I didn't know she lived in the Magic Realm then, of course. But that didn't matter. I had agreed to go wherever the little owl needed me to.

"And now here you are, Belladonna. Back where you belong." Aunt Hemlock grinned like a wolf as she paced up and down in front of me.

"There's one thing I still don't

understand," I said in a croaky voice. "Why do you want me here, Aunt Hemlock? You were the one who banished me in the first place. I might be your niece, but you don't even like me."

"Like you?" Aunt Hemlock stopped dead in her tracks and stared at me down her long warty nose. "What's that got to do with anything? Of course I don't like you. You're always so horribly cheerful – laughing and smiling with any little creature you happen to meet. I can't bear it."

"So why bring me back?" I asked.

"Because I need something from you, that's why." Aunt Hemlock's hand shot out. She grabbed me by the scruff of the neck and dragged me towards her broomstick.

"Wait!" I cried. "Where are we going? What is it you want from me?"

"You'll see soon enough!" Aunt Hemlock

leapt on board her broom and shot up into the air, still clutching me by the hood of my coat.

"Yikes!" I gasped.

"You better hold on tight," she shouted as I dangled beneath her like a fish on a hook.

I looked down and saw the sharp, jagged rocks poking out of the marsh beneath us. If I fell now, I would break every bone in my body. I grabbed hold of the slippery wooden broom handle and scrambled up behind Aunt Hemlock as we swooped away across the eerie green moonlit marsh.

"Slow down!" I begged as I clung on for dear life. I had no other choice. Wherever Aunt Hemlock and her broom were taking me, I would have to go.

Chapter Nine

Aunt Hemlock's broom shot through the air like a thunderbolt as I held on tightly behind her.

"Fizzing fire-dragons!" I cried. I had forgotten how fast she liked to fly, spinning in circles and turning loop-the-loops whenever I screamed.

"Where are we going?" I cried as icy hailstones flew in my face.

Aunt Hemlock ignored me and

corkscrewed so fast, I nearly fell off the broomstick completely. I was left clinging to the handle by nothing but the tips of my fingers as she swooped low over the marsh.

"Help!" I squealed, just managing to grab on with my other hand too.

Aunt Hemlock took no notice. She spun in a figure of eight and laughed. "Nearly there now. Don't you recognize it?"

I was so dizzy I could barely see straight, but as I blinked through the falling hailstones I began to spot familiar wind-bent trees and looming dark rocks on the gloomy marshland below.

"You're taking me to your cave," I groaned. I should have guessed.

Sure enough, a few moments later we flew over the patch of dark, squelchy bog where I had spent so many unhappy days and nights before I went to live in the Person World.

"Here we are!" she cackled. "Home sweet home!"

"No!" I said, as the broomstick landed and I fell backwards into a soggy heap in a puddle. "You can steal me away if you want to, Aunt Hemlock. But you can never make me call this horrible place my home!"

As I spoke, I saw a picture in my mind of Honeysuckle Cottage with its pretty little thatched roof and Rascal fast asleep on the sunny windowsill. That was my home – with Aunty Rose and Uncle Martin. Although they weren't there just now, of course. They were camping in the woods. They'd have no idea how to come and rescue me – or even where I had gone. My tummy twisted like a snake as I thought how scared they'd be when they woke up in the tent and found that I had vanished. Then I remembered my spell:

If you wake and I am gone,
Just keep calm and carry on!
Don't even notice I'm not here,
Until I'm back and reappear.

At least they wouldn't be anxious about me. My magic charm meant they'd think it was quite normal that I suddenly wasn't there. Except... A terrible thought struck me as I sat in the freezing bog-puddle with the icy black water chilling my bones. *Maybe I would never get back to the Person World at all. Then they wouldn't remember I had ever lived with them. They'd completely forget they had once fostered a girl named Bella.*

I staggered to my feet, but my tummy felt so tight I could barely stand.

"How could you do this to me, Aunt Hemlock?" I squelched to the edge of the puddle and glared at her. "I love it in the Person World. You know I do." As I glanced towards the pitch-black inky mouth of her cave, I could feel my cheeks burning with rage. "I'm not going to live in this horrible place with you. I'm not!"

Out of the corner of my eye, I saw the pale stony path that led away in the opposite direction, out over the windswept marshes towards the snowy mountains beyond.

Without thinking, I turned on my heel and ran – sprinting as fast as my cold, wet legs would take me.

"Oh no you don't! I've got plans for you!" Aunt Hemlock was back on her broomstick and flying beside me in a flash. She dug inside her cloak and pulled out her long, thin wand as she screeched a spell at the top of her voice:

> *Build a prison wall for me*
> *So this witch-child cannot flee.*

"No!" I cried.

But a shower of tiny sharp spikes shot over the top of my head as if it was raining nails. The stony path cracked open right ahead of me, and where the spikes landed, a thick thorn hedge instantly grew up out of the ground. I skidded to a stop just in time before I was cut to shreds. In an instant, the magic hedge was twice as tall as the top of my head. Each thorn was as long as my finger and as sharp as a spear. There was no way to get past the thick, deep,

prickly wall and escape. Not over it. Not under it. Not through it.

I was trapped.

I sunk to my knees. All my anger turned to frustration and a tear trickled down my cheek. "Oh, Aunty Rose. Uncle Martin." I sobbed, wandering if I would ever see them again.

"Ha!" Aunt Hemlock swooped down on me like a vampire bat. "That's it. That's what I wanted," she cried. She caught the tear on the end of wand and popped it into a glass jar which she pulled from beneath her cloak.

"Tears?" I said, blinking up at her. "You brought me here so you could take my tears?"

"Of course. The tears of a child are so

very useful for making spells," she said, catching another one as it rolled down my cheek. "I had a whole jarful from when you were a baby. You were always crying after your parents were foolish enough to turn themselves into white mice and get eaten by a cat."

So that's why Aunt Hemlock had agreed to take me in all those years ago – so she could steal my tears. I had always wondered why she bothered.

"All those baby tears have run out now," she said, shaking the jar. "I needed a top-up."

I sniffed as hard as I could and tried to stop any more tears rolling down my cheeks. I couldn't bear to think I was helping her in any way.

"Come on! Cry," she hissed. "I can't force you with magic. The tears have to flow by themselves or they're only half as good."

I bit my lip. I could have filled a bathtub with all the tears I wanted to let loose, but I wasn't going to let another drop fall from my eyes. Not if it would help Aunt Hemlock with her dreadful spells. She had row upon row of shelves inside her cave all filled with strange and horrible ingredients for potions that could do terrible things. I couldn't be part of it.

"Come on! Cry!" she urged again. "How am I supposed to make my famous Misery Mist if I don't have the tears of a child to add to the cauldron?"

"Misery Mist?" I gulped. I had seen that spell – a bubbling tombstone-grey liquid, one drop of which could reduce Aunt Hemlock's enemies to months of shoulder-shaking sobs. I remembered how she had used it once to punish a goblin who had accidentally picked a berry from one of her bushes. The poor little thing had cried so much, he couldn't see where he was going and constantly tripped over the roots of trees.

"And then of course, there is my lovely Lotion of Woe," said Aunt Hemlock, "and my precious Tincture of Despair. They both need lots of tears. Lots and lots. . ."

I had no idea what either of those potions did, but they both sounded horrible.

"No! I won't do it." I picked myself up from the ground and shook my head. "If that's what you want, you've wasted your time bringing me here, Aunt Hemlock," I said firmly. "I will not give you my tears. Not a single one."

Chapter Ten

I dried my eyes on my sleeve, making sure that no more tears escaped and rolled down my cheeks.

"Suit yourself, Belladonna! I can wait," hissed Aunt Hemlock. "You'll cry soon enough. You'll get homesick for that disgusting pretty little cottage and those silly Persons you love so much."

She was right, of course. I had only been back in the Magic Realm for less than an hour and I already missed the Person World almost more than I could bear. But even if I cried a bucketful of tears, I couldn't trust Aunt Hemlock to let me go.

"If you're going to be so stubborn, you can at least make yourself useful while we wait," she sighed. "I have plenty of chores you can be getting on with."

"Chores?" I said, looking up at the moonlit sky. "But it's the middle of the night."

"Exactly." She grinned. "Let's see how tearful you feel without a wink of sleep. I'm off for a nap. You can stay awake and cook some porridge for my breakfast. Make sure it's lovely and lumpy. Just the way I like it."

"Yes, Aunt Hemlock," I said with a deep sigh. There was no point in arguing. Pleading with her to let me go would be no more use than trying to squeeze through the towering hedge of thorns she had magicked-up to trap me here. Nor would losing my temper and screaming at her. Whatever happened, I didn't want to make Aunt Hemlock any more angry than she already was or she might turn me into a toad — or a slug (that was one of her favourite punishments). I was determined, one way or another, to get back to the Person World. When I did finally find a way to escape from this horrible place, I didn't want to be a tiny slug, so small and slimy that Aunty Rose and Uncle Martin might step on me without even knowing I was there.

"What are you grinning at?" barked Aunt Hemlock.

"Nothing!" I said quickly. But I realized I was smiling to myself. Even the thought of getting home had made me feel better.

All I needed was a little time to come up with a plan.

"Hmm!" Aunt Hemlock poked me with her wand. "Get back to the cave," she ordered. "My clever thorn hedge means you can't go more than three hundred paces from the door. And there's no way to get through it, so don't even try."

"Yes, Aunt Hemlock," I said as I trudged back along the path towards the small boggy clearing outside her cavern.

"There's no way out of here. Not unless you can do magic, of course," she added, howling with laughter as if she had made a very funny joke. "But you can't do magic, can you, Belladonna? You don't even have a wand, do you? Not since I threw it away when I banished you the Person World."

"That's right," I whispered, truthfully. "You did throw away my old wand." It was a horrible splintery thing that had turned into an angry rat and scampered off into a bush.

"It was pointless you even having a magic wand," cackled Aunt Hemlock. "It's not as if you could ever do anything with it. Not a single spell you ever did went right. You always were such a hopeless witch."

"Yes, Aunt Hemlock, that's what you've always told me," I said meekly. But I slipped my hand inside my pocket and touched the soft fluffy feathers of my magical flamingo pen. Aunt Hemlock had no idea that I had a wonderful new wand now or that I could do brilliant magical things with it, which I could never have dreamed of before.

It was my secret – just as long as she never found out. I felt a real glimmer of hope rising inside me for the first time since I'd arrived in this horrible place. I had my wand – perhaps I could find a way to use magic to help me escape.

"Get on and make my porridge," Aunt Hemlock barked, pointing towards a big iron cauldron hanging over a blackened cooking pit outside the door to the cave. "You'll need to fetch the wood and make a fire first." She stretched her spindly arms and yawned. "I'll want my breakfast as soon as I wake up."

"Of course, Aunt Hemlock," I said.

But as she stalked off into the cave, I touched the soft feathers of my wand again and my freezing fingers tingled with excitement.

I wasn't a hopeless witch – not any more. I bit my lip and nodded with determination. I was good at magic now and I would use it to find a way to escape.

As soon as I could hear Aunt Hemlock's snores coming from inside the cave, I tiptoed across the soggy clearing in the opposite direction to where I had seen the thorny hedge spring up. Perhaps the pathway down there was still clear.

Whoa!

I should have known better.

I skidded to a stop at the edge of the bog as I came face to face with the same thick wall of spiky thorns.

I turned and ran in a third direction – then a fourth. Each time the tall, prickly hedge blocked my way.

Aunt Hemlock must have made a circle of thorns in a ring all around the boggy land at the edge of her cave. Three hundred steps in each direction . . . that was it! There was no way out.

"Fine! Have it your way, then," I said and I slipped my wand out of my pocket at last.

My hands were shaking as I glanced over my shoulder to check Aunt Hemlock was still safely inside her cave. I pricked my ears as her loud snores echoed across the clearing. "Here goes." I raised my arm and I whispered my spell:

Let me pass through this thorny wall
I don't belong in this place at all!

A gentle haze of magic glistened in the air for a moment like pink raindrops. I held my breath — would my little spell be powerful enough to work against the wicked sorcery of this strange dark hedge. . .?

Ping!

A shower of thorns shot out of the hedge at me like arrows.

Ping! Ping! Ping!

"Stop!" I cried, ducking down and shielding my face as I waved my wand again.

Please don't tear and rip and scratch,

I must escape this awful patch!

It was hopeless. The thorns were flying around my head now and I saw that they had each grown a set of tiny wings.

Buzzzzz! Buzzzzzzzz! Buzzzzzzzzz!

I turned and fled as the angry thorns pursued me back along the path like a swarm of wasps.

They chased me three times in a circle around the soggy clearing outside the cave, until I slipped and landed – bottom first – right inside the giant cooking pot. Nothing but my arms and legs were poking out.

For ten whole minutes, I lay like a tortoise stuck on its back rocking from side to side, trying to get my wedged bottom out of the cauldron. The flying thorns were finally gone, at least, and Aunt Hemlock hadn't woken up. I could still hear her snoring

like a giant troll inside the cave — but by the time I was free, I could already see the cold, grey dawn creeping over the horizon.

"It's not fair! I want to go home," I whispered, feeling utterly defeated. But I refused to cry — not a single tear would fall from my eyes while I was still in the Magic Realm. I couldn't risk it. Aunt Hemlock might suddenly appear and use them for her dreadful potions. I couldn't allow that to happen, no matter how sad I felt.

Yet it was hard not to just sit down and weep. I had hoped so much that magic would help me escape, but I was still stuck here — at least until I thought of another way to break through the enchanted ring of thorns. And if I didn't make Aunt Hemlock's horrid lumpy porridge by the time she woke up, things would be far worse.

Chapter Eleven

The first thing I needed to do if I was going to make Aunt Hemlock's porridge was to build a fire.

I sighed as I saw an enormous pile of wood on the far side of the clearing by the well. As I began to drag the heavy logs over to the cooking pit, I thought fondly of the clever little camping stove Aunty Rose had used to make our supper last night.

"Now that's *real* magic!" I said, cheering up just a tiny bit as I imagined how jealous Aunt Hemlock would be if she could see half the cunning things Persons take on camping trips to make their life easy.

"Rumbling rhinos," I gasped, almost dropping a huge hefty log on my foot. "I could certainly make this job a lot easier for myself, if I tried!" I might not know a spell strong enough to break through the wall of thorns, but I didn't need to carry these heavy logs when a little magic could do the work for me.

Aunt Hemlock's snores were still echoing out of the cave, so I pulled my wand from my pocket and quickly muttered a spell.

Please help me, kind wood,
Make a fire if you could.

I wasn't sure the little chant would do anything – not after my disastrous attempt to break through Aunt Hemlock's thorny prison. Perhaps my magic just wasn't strong enough to work in this dreadful place at all.

But I was amazed to see my flamingo wand sparkle brightly in the gloom. I still had magic power after all!

I gave a little grin of pride as the logs got up and began to float towards the fire pit. They piled themselves up one on top of the other in a neat pyramid and – before I even asked – crackling orange flames were dancing with warmth and a delicious smell of woodsmoke filled the air.

"Well done!" I whispered, my spirits lifting a little as I ran my fingers over the soft feathers of my wand. The fire looked so jolly and bright in the cold, grey light. I held my hands up for a moment or two and warmed them. Then I turned towards the big black cooking pot.

"Now you!" I said firmly with a flick of my wand.

Please cook some porridge thick and hot. . .

"Erm..!" I stopped halfway through as I tried to think of a rhyme to end my spell. Magic always works better if you say it in rhyme.

"Ah! Got it," I whispered under my breath.

Please cook some porridge thick and hot . . .
Make it gooey and lumpy like
horrid troll snot!

That sounded just about right for the revolting wobbly frogspawn mixture Aunt Hemlock always likes to eat for her breakfast. A shower of pink sparks shot out of the end of my wand. They looked so pretty that they seemed quite out of place in the damp, dark swamp – like dragonflies or sparkly jewels lighting up the gloom. It didn't seem at all the right sort of magic to make a witch's porridge. But the pot leapt up on top of the flames and began to bubble merrily.

Pop! Pop! Pop!

I peeped over the top and saw a thick, steaming goo.

"Perfect!" I said with a grin. Then, feeling a fresh sense of hope, I sat down to warm myself by the fire for a moment or two while I tried to make a new plan of how my magic might help me to escape before Aunt Hemlock woke up.

I stared into the bright dancing flames, thinking how pretty they were. My eyes felt heavy and I yawned as I watched the shimmering flecks of red and orange and blue and gold. My eyes felt heavier still. Heavier and heavier...

"BELLADONNA BROOMSTICK!"

I must have fallen asleep because the next thing I knew, it was morning and Aunt Hemlock was standing over me, shouting at the top of her voice.

"What is the meaning of this?" she roared.

I blinked sleepily. Looking down I saw that I was still clutching my pink flamingo wand. I stuffed it into my pocket, hoping Aunt Hemlock hadn't noticed. She was staring into the bubbling cauldron. I was a little worried to see a curling trail of pretty rainbow-coloured smoke coming out of the top – and the pot was rocking from side to side, making a sort of merry giggling sound as if it was full of popping candy. That didn't seem quite right. But I crossed my fingers and hoped for the best.

"That's your breakfast, Aunt Hemlock," I said brightly. "You know, nice lumpy porridge. Just the way you like it!"

"This is NOT the way I like my porridge!" thundered Aunt Hemlock and she plunged a ladle into the pot. "Just look at it!"

"Flittering fairies!" I gasped with surprise. "It's bright pink!"

"Exactly!" growled Aunt Hemlock. "Horribly, horribly pink! I have never see anything so disgustingly pretty in all my life! And what in the name of toad's toenails are those?" She held the gently popping ladle under my nose and pointed a crooked finger at something small and soft floating in the rose-pink porridge.

As a waft of sweet strawberry-scented steam filled my nose, I couldn't help but smile.

"I think those are marshmallows, Aunt Hemlock," I said. "Heart-shaped ones!"

"Marshmallows?" Aunt Hemlock looked as if she might explode.

"You should try one," I said. "They're delicious — sort of gooey like sugar clouds." But as I spoke, the smile faded on my lips. Something had gone terribly wrong with my spell. I had been swept away for a moment by the sweet smells coming from the cooking pot. But I knew the Magic Realm was no place for pretty pink porridge or fluffy marshmallows. And Aunt Hemlock did not look pleased.

She sniffed the porridge again and her long

nose wrinkled. "I smell magic. Someone has cast a spell on my breakfast," she roared.

"Really?" I tried my best to sound surprised, but my heart was beating so loudly I felt sure Aunt Hemlock would hear it pounding inside my chest.

Her narrow eyes were glistening in the light of the fire as she shook her head in disbelief.

"Has someone come near the cave?" she roared. "Old Mother Newtbreath, perhaps? She has always been jealous of my power. Or Wizard Darklore? Come out, come out, wherever you are."

There was no answer, of course.

Aunt Hemlock scratched her chin. She seemed lost for words for a moment. Then she swivelled round, very slowly and stared at me.

"You!" she said, pointing her finger

in disbelief. "You did this, Belladonna. Nobody else would turn my porridge such a disgusting shade of pink. You've been using magic, haven't you?"

"Me?" I said, feeling my cheeks burning hotter than the flickering flames. "How could I do magic?" I stuffed my hands deep into my pockets. If Aunt Hemlock found out I had a new wand, she'd take it away and I would never get the chance to try and escape ever again.

But Aunt Hemlock is like a hawk. She sees everything.

Her bony hand gripped my shoulder. "What's that you're hiding in your coat?" she hissed. "Empty your pockets."

"My pockets?" I quivered.

"Yes," said Aunt Hemlock. "Empty them. Right now!"

I bit my lip to stop myself from screaming

out loud. It was all over. If Aunt Hemlock found my wand, then my only chance of escaping from this place was gone for ever.

Chapter Twelve

Aunt Hemlock grabbed me by the scruff of the neck.

"This way!" she said and she marched me into her cave. A lantern full of trapped fireflies glowed above the big stone slab she used as a table to make her dreadful potions on. I looked at the shelves all around the walls, crammed-full of glass jars and bottles. There were horrible things arranged in every direction, like Itchy Pox Powder made from poison ivy and viper spit. Just one pinch could send a victim mad with itching, until they pulled their own hair from their scalp. Or Bitterness Water, brewed from the ground-down bones of wicked highwaymen. One splash could make an unsuspecting creature turn with hate against the thing they most loved. I'd once seen a mother vulture abandon her nest of eggs after just a single drop of the liquid touched her beak.

How many of these wicked mixtures contain tears? I wondered.

I was staring hard at the potions, thinking how I'd like to destroy them all for ever, when I jumped with fright. Aunt Hemlock's horrible chameleon, Wane, had appeared suddenly amongst the  bottles and jars. "Hello, Belladonna! Fancy seeing you here," he sneered, as he scuttled out of the gloom and climbed on to Aunt Hemlock's shoulder.

I've always hated the way I never know where he is going to turn up next. He can vanish and materialize again like mist. But it wasn't the creepy shape-shifting lizard that was making my knees tremble – nor the terrible potions. It was the thought that Aunt Hemlock might take away my magic flamingo pen. Without it, I would never be able to escape from this dreadful place. If that came true, I wouldn't be able to help myself. I would cry a well full of tears, enough for Aunt Hemlock to make her terrible potions until the end of time.

"Empty your pockets," she said, slapping her hand down on the cold stone surface of the table. "You've got a wand in there somewhere. I'm sure of it."

I had no choice. With shaking fingers, I began with my left pocket first. The one without my wand in it.

There was one white tissue (crumpled but clean), one sucky sweet in a purple wrapper (I didn't even know I had that) and the funny green frog torch Uncle Martin had given me.

"Hmm!" Aunt Hemlock picked the frog up by its little plastic foot.

"It's not even real," tittered Wane.

"What's the point in that?" growled Aunt Hemlock. "Who wants a frog you can't throw into a potion?"

I was about to explain that it was a torch, but she was already clicking her fingers impatiently.

"And the other pocket. Empty that one too."

"Hurry up. Do as you're told," hissed Wane, licking his lips.

I found an old bus ticket and laid that on the table, smoothing it out carefully as I played for time. Then I dipped my hand into my pocket again. I knew there was nothing else left except my magic pink pen. There was no point in hiding it – Aunt Hemlock would only turn my pockets out herself.

"Hurry up!" she said, taking a step closer.

I laid my precious wand on the table and held my breath.

"Ah-ha! What's this, then?" Aunt Hemlock's hand shot out, grabbing hold of a feather and dangling the pretty pen out in front of her with a look of disgust. "It's revoltingly pink, whatever it is."

"Revolting," agreed Wane.

"Er... It's just a ... a thingamajig." My mind was whirring. At least Aunt Hemlock hadn't recognized it as a wand right away. "It's a ... a pen!" I said truthfully.

"Like a quill?" Aunt Hemlock wrinkled her nose.

"Exactly like a quill," I said, quickly. "Only you don't need to dip it in ink all the time. I use it for writing and drawing and things..."

"Hmm." Aunt Hemlock grinned as she took hold of a scrap of parchment and wrote something across the top of it in her thin scratchy writing:

Chores I Need To Do Today

Then she underlined it – three times – and waved the pen in the air.

For a terrible moment I thought magic sparks might shoot out of the end if she swished it about like that. But nothing happened, thank goodness. Aunt Hemlock chewed her lip and made a great show of mumbling under her breath.

"Now, what chores *do* I need to do today? I really *should* make a list."

Wane began to giggle. "Oh, mistress, you are funny."

I didn't see the joke.

Not until Aunt Hemlock threw back her head and cackled with laughter too. "Of course, I don't need to worry about chores any more, do I, Belladonna? Not now I've got you to do them for me."

I should have known it was me they were laughing at. But I lifted my head and smiled as brightly as I could. They were probably just trying to make me cry. I would not do that.

"How about I get started right away," I said, eagerly. "Do you want me to sweep the floor first? Or maybe I could scrub out your cauldron?" If Aunt Hemlock was thinking about chores she needed doing, she might forget about hunting for my wand. "I really could write a list if you like and make sure everything gets done." I held out my hand hoping she would pass me back my pen.

But, before either of us could say another word, there was a high-pitched hooting sound and a flash of feathers as a tiny owl shot out of the darkness at the back of the cave.

"Little Woo!" I gasped. I hadn't even realized she was in here. She must live in the cave with Aunt Hemlock as well — probably sucking up to her all the time just like Wane.

She swooped down and grabbed a beakful of pink feathers from Aunt

Hemlock's outstretched hand.

"Stop!" I cried, staring in horror as she snatched my one chance of escape. I leapt in air, trying to reach her and grab the tip of my wand. But the little owl shot out of the cave and flew away with my magical flamingo pen clamped firmly in her beak.

"Give that back to me!" I wailed, dashing to the door.

"Oh, do be quiet! You're screeching like

a banshee," Aunt Hemlock snapped.

Little Woo had disappeared into the clouds.

"There's no point in making a fuss. You'll never see your . . . what was it called? Pen – ever again." Aunt Hemlock shrugged. "That feather-brained owl will rip it to shreds. She seems to think it is a fluffy pink mouse."

Aunt Hemlock and Wane laughed again, as if this was hilarious. But I could barely swallow.

"Please come back," I called weakly. But the owl was long gone.

She had taken my precious feathery pen with her. Aunt Hemlock was right, Little Woo had probably ripped it to shreds already.

I would never see my wonderful wand again. And I would never escape from here without it.

Chapter Thirteen

I was still staring out into the grey morning clouds, hopelessly searching through the rain for any sign of Little Woo and my stolen wand, when there was a flash of light in the cave behind me. I heard Aunt Hemlock gasp with surprise.

I spun round and saw that she was holding the little plastic frog in her outstretched hand. As she squeezed its legs, another flash of bright light filled the gloomy cave. "Well,

well?" she cackled excitedly. "What have we here?"

"It's only a torch," I said as Aunt Hemlock prodded the frog with the tip of her wand.

"Nonsense," she growled, waving the shimmering light around. "This is magic."

"That's right!" agreed Wane. "Do you think Belladonna put a hex on that frog? It was in her pocket after all?" He took a step back as if he was afraid I might suddenly start doing spells on shape-shifting lizards like him.

I shook my head. "It's not magic. It's just a Person thing. It creates its own electricity when you squeeze the plastic frog legs together," I explained. "See ..." I reluctantly stepped away from the door of the cave, giving up all hope of ever seeing my wand again, and took the torch from Aunt Hemlock's hand. "If you pump really hard, the light comes on. That's why it doesn't need batteries."

"Batteries?" Aunt Hemlock looked confused.

"Oh, you know ... little pods of power." Explaining even the simplest things from the Person World was so hard.

"Liar," barked Aunt Hemlock. She snatched the torch back. "I know magic when I see it, child. You have enchanted this frog and made it your wand." She flashed the light across the walls of the cave.

I could see why she might think that. Most witches' wands bear close association to one animal or another. My old one was a rat – and then there was my precious flamingo, of course. So why not a frog? But in this case Aunt Hemlock was wrong. The magic she saw was simply a clever invention from the Person World.

"I promise you, it's only a torch," I said. "It's a bit like a candle, or a lantern. Except there's no flame."

"A candle with no flame?" Aunt Hemlock scratched her head suspiciously. "That can't be right. You're tricking me, Belladonna."

"No," I said, "I'm not." But she waved the torch in the air muttering under her breath.

Oh little frog who came from a pond,
Show me a spell, now you're a wand.

There were no sparks or puffs of smoke, of course, just a shimmer of torchlight. Aunt Hemlock was grinding her teeth and I could tell she was getting angrier and angrier as she couldn't understand what made the little frog glow.

Wane, meanwhile, was jumping up and down, trying to catch the dancing light on walls, just as Rascal would if I was playing with a torch at home.

"You are wise and clever, Mistress. It is definitely a magic wand," he said.

"Exactly. I've had enough of this." Aunt Hemlock grabbed me by the elbow and marched me outside to where the strawberry-scented porridge pot was still bubbling merrily above the fire. "Show me how you turned my breakfast so horribly, horribly pink!" she commanded. "Go on! Turn it nice and grey again, just like it should be – or a lovely mouldy green – with proper lumps." She slapped the little plastic torch into my hand. "Do it or I'll turn you into a slug!"

I knew it wouldn't be long before she threatened me with her favourite slug punishment. She used to turn me into a slug at least once a month when I lived here before. Crawling around on my belly eating nothing but raw cabbage for days on end was something I never wanted to do again. Not to mention all that sluggy-slime. There was also a strange, sad, damp feeling that always came over me whenever I was a slug.

"Well?" Aunt Hemlock's fingers were twitching with anticipation.

"I can't do anything to change the porridge," I said, helplessly. "I've told you. This isn't my wand."

"It must be." Aunt Hemlock snatched the torch back again. "How else does it shine like that? And don't give me any of your nonsense about batteroos..."

"Batteries?" I said, trying to be helpful.

But Aunt Hemlock was leaning over the cauldron, shining the torchlight inside.

Stupid frog-wand. Do as you're told,
  Turn this porridge the colour of mould!

Still, nothing happened. She leant in even closer. With just one little push, I could have sent her tumbling head first into the bubbling pot. But even if she exploded like a giant witch-sized lump of popping candy, it would do no good. Little Woo had taken my real wand and flown away. Without that to help me escape, I'd still be stuck here — trapped for ever on the wrong side of Aunt Hemlock's magic ring of thorns.

"I know an enchantment when I see one, Belladonna," she said, straightening up with a look of fury on her steaming-hot face. "You won't be getting this silly frog wand of yours back again." She slipped the torch into the pocket of her long black cloak. "I'm off to get myself a decent witching breakfast at the Clanking Cauldron Cafe. Old Mother Bubblepot makes a fine scrambled snake egg on mouldy toadstool toast."

She put her fingers to her mouth and whistled. Her battered broomstick came shooting out of the cave and hovered just above the ground so she could climb on board.

"Wait for me, Mistress!" Wane clung to the hem of her cloak as the broom rose up. "Can I have a squashed fly muffin for my breakfast?" he begged, licking his lips as he scuttled on to her shoulder.

"We'll see," said Aunt Hemlock as they circled above me. "As for you, Belladonna – you can scrub out that cauldron and get rid of that foul pink muck while we're gone."

"Won't be much fun. Not without your little froggy wand to help you!" hissed Wane.

"It is *not* my wand. It's just a torch," I

said for the hundredth time. But he was right about one thing – the pink porridge had been cooking for so long it had gone as gluey as bubblegum. Cleaning out the enormous cauldron was going to be a horrible job. It would probably take me all morning.

"Oh, I almost forgot!" Aunt Hemlock grinned so widely, her jagged green teeth showed. "I've made a little note of a few other chores I'd like you to do too. Such a pity the owl stole your pen or you could have ticked each one off the list as you went along." She took a curly roll of yellowy-brown parchment from the end of her sleeve and unrolled it with a flourish. "I'm going to brew a few little potions later, you see."

"Potions?" My heart began to pound. If Aunt Hemlock was getting ready to make a horrible witchy brew, that could only mean one thing. She would want my tears to help her.

LIST OF JOBS FOR BELLADONNA

i. Scrub Cauldron
ii. Scrub it again - PROPERLY
iii. Fill a jar with frogspawn from the bog
iv. Fill six more jars with toad spawn too
v. Catch a scream and trap it in a net
vi. Find the tongue of an adder and

The broomstick was hovering high above my head by now, but the parchment was so long it reached right down to the ground – and even dragged along it. I couldn't read everything. But I saw that the last number on the list was 101. How many horrible potions did Aunt Hemlock want to make?

"There's a-hundred-and-one jobs here," I gasped. "I can't do all those, Aunt Hemlock. Not before you're back from breakfast."

"Oh dear, oh dear!" She threw her head back and laughed as she dropped the scroll on the ground beside me. "You look as if you might be about to cry, Belladonna."

"I'm not!" I said firmly.

"Good." She laughed again. "Save your tears ... I'll be wanting them later."

Chapter Fourteen

After Aunt Hemlock had flown away on her broomstick, I unrolled the scroll of chores again and groaned at how long and difficult-looking it was.

"Labouring lizards!" I gasped. All these jobs would take a hundred years, not just one single morning – even if I did have a magic wand to help me. Which I didn't, of course. Not since Little Woo had stolen it and flown away.

I ran my eyes down the list and stopped at job number 8:

Harvest snarflebung root and crush to fine powder

"What in the name of slippery serpents is snarflebung root?" I asked a tiny spider, swinging behind me from the doorway of Aunt Hemlock's cave. Was it something to eat? Or was it part of some terrible potion too?

"Sorry. Haven't a clue," said the spider, shrugging four of his eight little legs and swinging away as fast as he could.

He was probably wise to run off. As I glanced further down the list, I saw that Job Number 19 was to squash a pound of spiders to make an ointment.

Small ones are best! Aunt Hemlock had advised.

"Don't worry, Mr Spider," I called after him. "I won't do that to you, no matter what." But Job Number 27 sounded truly disgusting:

Scrub the walls of the cave with bog water and toad spit

Number 64 might be even worse . . . Aunt Hemlock wanted me to wash her underwear in the swamp! And Number 83 was just plain dangerous:

Collect one nose hair from a fire-breathing dragon

I glanced back to the top of the list. Perhaps scrubbing out the cauldron wouldn't be such a terrible place to start after all. At least I had some idea what I was supposed

to do even without magic to help me ...
no poor little spiders would be harmed and
the cauldron *probably* wouldn't eat me alive.

No matter how gloomy I felt about being
trapped here in the Magic Realm, or losing
my wand, or the mountain of chores in
front of me, there was no point in putting
it off any longer. If I hadn't even made a
start by the time Aunt Hemlock got home,
she would turn me into a slug for sure.

"Scrubbing the cauldron can do no real
harm," I told myself.

At least while I was doing that, I wasn't
actually gathering any of the ingredients
for her sinister potions yet.

I found an old piece of sacking to use
like a pair of oven gloves and lifted the
enormous cauldron off the fire. The huge
iron pot was as heavy as a baby giant and
as hot as a dragon's egg, but I managed to

stumble to the edge of the swamp and cool it down in the murky green water.

Half an hour later, I was still scrubbing sticky pink goo off the inside of the pot. Whatever the magic porridge had been made of, it wasn't going to shift easily.

My arms ached as if I'd been mud wrestling with a troll. I had bog mud under my fingernails and swamp weed in my hair. It was raining again – thin, cold drizzle – but I was so wet already, I barely even noticed.

Hard as I tried to keep cheerful, I couldn't stop thinking about the Person World – about wonderful things like dishwashers and bubbly washing-up liquid and warm water ... but most of all, I thought about Uncle Martin and Aunty Rose. We didn't have a fancy dishwasher like Piers's family, so we usually all did the washing up together after dinner. Uncle Martin liked to wash — and always made a sort of silly Father Christmas beard out of the bubbles. It made me laugh every time. I did the drying — with a nice clean tea-towel which smelled of lavender-scented washing powder — and Aunty Rose put everything away, singing cheerful songs out of tune as she went ... and she always had to ask Uncle Martin to reach the tall cupboard where the glasses are kept.

Who would have thought I could miss washing up? It was impossible to believe I had only been back in this terrible place for one night. How could so much change in such a tiny space of time?

"Rotten rats! It's just not fair," I groaned, sticking my head inside the cauldron again and scrubbing at the base with a soggy scrap of spongy bog weed. Perhaps I should just give in and cry. I could fill this giant cauldron with all the precious tears Aunt Hemlock wanted.

Suddenly there was a loud clang as something hard hit the outside of the huge iron pot. I lifted my head and gasped with surprise as I saw Little Woo hovering above me.

Lying there, right beside the cauldron, was my pink flamingo pen. "My wand!" I cried. "You brought it back."

I was stunned. Why was the little owl helping me?

"Twit-woo." She landed on a mossy rock close by and stared up at me with her big yellow eyes.

"Thank you, Little Woo." As I darted forward and grabbed the wand, I saw that it was as good as new. She hadn't ripped it to shreds with her beak like Aunt Hemlock had said she would. In fact, it didn't even look as if she'd so much as pecked it.

"You kept it safe," I said.

"Of course," hooted Little Woo. She hopped closer. "I knew it was special to you, Bella. I wanted to protect it for you so Aunt Hemlock couldn't take it away."

"But..." I shook my head. "I thought you were on her side. I thought you were one of her magic pets, like Wane. I thought you did everything she told you to."

"No!" Little Woo fluttered over to the edge of the cauldron, so that she was perching right beside my hand. "I did trick you into coming here, Bella. I wish I hadn't done that. But Aunt Hemlock said if I brought you to the Magic Realm, then she would let me go back to my own family in return."

I saw a dark shadow of sadness pass over

Little Woo's bright eyes. "But I don't think she's going to do that," she hooted. "I think she lied."

"Oh, Woo. She tricked you too!" I sighed.

"Yes," hooted the tiny owl as I stroked her feathers. "I have to stay here and deliver messages for her wherever she asks me to. But I just hope I don't ever have to do anything as terrible as I did to you again."

"Why don't you fly away?" I asked. "Is the wall of thorns stopping you too?"

She shook her head.

"Then escape from here. Go back to your family by yourself," I cried.

"I can't. I don't know where they live," said Little Woo, in a voice so soft I could barely hear her. "Aunt Hemlock stole me from my nest when I was just a tiny fledgling. I had only hatched out of my egg a few days earlier. I didn't even know how to fly then and I was too young to remember my way back home."

"Oh, Woo!" I said, holding out my arm so that she could hop up on to my shoulder. "That's terrible." I couldn't think of anything more wicked than snatching a helpless new-hatched chick away from its parents.

"The only thing I remember," said Woo, "is that our nest was in an old hollow tree in the woods. And I had a brother and a sister. But I shouldn't think they even remember me. Nor my mum and dad either."

"Of course they'll remember you, Little Woo! No parent ever forgets their child," I said. And I was sure that was true.

"What will I do, Bella?" she hooted. "There must be thousands of hollow trees in the Magic Realm. How will I ever find the right one?"

"I don't know!" I said. There was no point in pretending it was going to be an easy task. "But I am going help you find that tree and get you back to your family somehow, Little Woo. I promise." I touched my heart to show her how serious I was. "My foster parents once told me how important it is for a Person to keep their word."

"Really?" The tiny owl nibbled my ear. "You'd do that for me, Bella. Even after I tricked you into coming here?"

"Of course," I said. "I know now that wasn't your fault. And you did a wonderful thing for me too. You kept my wand safe!"

I was determined to repay her kindness and waved the feathery pink pen triumphantly in the air. As if to celebrate, a sparkly shower of tiny magic stars glistered against the endless grey drizzle for a moment.

"We're going to need this precious wand, Little Woo!" I said. "We're going to use it to help us both escape from Aunt Hemlock for ever."

Chapter Fifteen

I stood in front of the towering wall of spiky thorns, staring up at the giant hedge that surrounded us.

"There has to be a way to get through and escape before Aunt Hemlock comes back from breakfast," I told Little Woo as she perched on my shoulder. "Once we're free I can help you find your family, then I can try and get back to the Person World and join mine."

I thought with a fresh pang of Aunty Rose and Uncle Martin at the campsite in the woods.

"Use your wand," said Little Woo, excitedly pecking at the pink feathers. "Break the hedge down with witchy magic. *Pow! Pow! Pow!*"

"I've tried before," I said, feeling nervous as I remembered how the thorns had turned into angry wasps and chased me back to the cave. "Aunt Hemlock used a very powerful spell to make this hedge grow up so tall and fast. I'm not sure any magic of mine is strong enough to break it down again."

"Then what are you going to do?" asked Little Woo, panic rising in her voice. "Aunt Hemlock might come back at any moment."

"I don't know," I said, but my brain was whirring like a spinning wheel. There had to be some way that my magic could help me. I watched as Little Woo flapped her wings and rose up into the air, checking the skies for any sign of an approaching broomstick. She flew right up over the top of the hedge. The wall of thorns didn't stop her. She was allowed to come and go as she pleased in case she needed to deliver a message.

"That's it," I said, watching as she flapped her wings high above the thorns. "I might not know a spell strong enough to destroy the hedge, but I could use magic to make myself fly over it just like you're doing now."

"On a witch's broomstick?" hooted Little Woo, circling back towards me.

"No." I shook my head. I didn't have a broom with me. And Aunt Hemlock was using hers. "What I need is wings," I said. "Magic ones!" I held up my wand and grinned.

"Oooh!" hooted Little Woo. "Turn yourself into an owl like me. Then you'll have wonderful wings."

"Just what I was thinking," I agreed. Transforming into different animals is one of my favourite kinds of magic. I began to mutter a spell.

Give me wings like Little Woo
Then I'll be an owl and fly like
her t—

But in the split-second before I waved my wand, I stopped.

"Halt the magic!" I cried as a shower of sparks spluttered and fell uselessly to the ground. I looked at Little Woo and thought how soft and fluffy the baby owlet was. If my spell didn't work and I plunged down into the middle of the thorn bush, I'd want something far stronger than downy owl feathers to protect me.

"I need tougher wings than yours, Little Woo," I said, stroking her gently as she landed on my shoulder again.

"Tougher wings than an owl?" Little Woo sounded offended. "It's not possible . . . unless you're going to be a leathery old bat or something."

"A bat would be good," I said slowly. "You're right, their leathery wings would protect me from the thorns."

But I'd had an even better idea. I was staring down at the list of chores Aunt Hemlock had written for me. I'd dropped the scroll at my feet when Woo and I came to examine the hedge. With all the numbers written down the side like that, it reminded me of the takeaway food menus we have stuck on the fridge at Honeysuckle Cottage.

Aunty Rose likes pizza best. Uncle Martin prefers Indian curry. But Chinese food is my favourite. We have takeaways sometimes on Friday nights as a treat. All we have to do is phone the restaurant, order any number we want, and they deliver it.

My favourite Chinese dish of all is Number 29.

"Sweet and sour chicken," I said out loud.

"You're going to be a chicken?" squawked Little Woo, almost toppling over backwards. "I've never heard anything so silly. Owl feathers are far stronger than any soppy old chicken. Chickens can't even fly properly."

"Don't worry," I laughed. "I am definitely not going to be a chicken." I glanced at the list of chores again, reading down through the numbers exactly like I would on a takeaway menu. "I am going to be number eighty-three today!" I said with a grin.

"Number eighty three?" Little Woo flew down from my shoulder and landed on the list. "Which one's that?" She pecked at the numbers furiously. But it didn't help. She still couldn't read them.

"Here," I said, crouching beside her and pointing to the right line. "Number eighty-three." I read Aunt Hemlock's instructions aloud. *"Collect one nose hair from a fire-breathing dragon."*

"Ah!" said Little Woo wisely. Then she shook her head in confusion. "How is turning yourself into a dragon's nose hair going to help you fly over the hedge?"

"Oh, Woo!" I giggled. "I'm not just going to be a dragon's nose hair!" I took a deep breath and tried not to laugh. She looked so cross and muddled. "I'm going to be the whole dragon," I explained.

"Oh!" Little Woo's wide eyes grew wider than ever. "A whole actual, real dragon?"

"Yes," I said, feeling nervous flames of excitement tickle my tummy. This might just work. Perhaps there really was a way I could escape from Aunt Hemlock's prison of thorns and help Little Woo find her family too.

I raised my wand in the air again and counted to three.

"I am going to turn myself into an actual, real dragon," I said. "A big red fire-breathing one. With wings!"

Chapter Sixteen

My hand was shaking as I raised my wand above my head. I have turned myself into lots of different animals before – one of the best ever was a black cat on Halloween. But I have never attempted anything as huge or magnificent as a dragon.

"Here goes!" I said as Little Woo circled above me. "Just make sure you grab my wand as soon as the spell is done. I'll throw it in the air for you to look after. I don't want to accidentally burn it to a crisp, the moment I turn into a fire-breathing dragon."

"Oh dear," hooted Little Woo nervously. "Oh dear. Oh dear."

"It'll be all right," I promised. It had to be! There wasn't a moment to lose. Aunt Hemlock could be back at any second. Before I could change my mind, I waved my wand and muttered a spell.

Make me a fiery dragon of the sky
With mighty wings to fly, fly, fly!

Whoosh!
No sooner were the words spoken, than

red-hot flames seemed to burn inside my chest. My belly was hotter than a cauldron and my heart felt like a glowing coal.

"It's happening!" I cried, tossing my wand in the air for Woo to catch. "Look after that. I'll need it to turn myself back into a girl again." But all I heard was a deafening dragon roar where my own voice was supposed to be.

"Twit-tu-WHOA!" Poor Little Woo hooted in panic as she grabbed the wand and flew up to the high branches of a tree.

I could feel a sharp tingling in my toes, like when you dip your feet in a bath that's too hot. I glanced down. Instead of the bright yellow wellies I had been wearing since the camping trip, I could see clawed feet with magnificent gold talons and red leathery skin like a crocodile. I stretched my neck as I looked up again and realized

I was so huge and tall, I could almost see over the top of the thorn hedge already. I could feel wings sprouting on my long back too — it was a sort of ticklish feeling, not really painful at all. I tried to turn around, with a great booming stride, and caught sight of my reflection in the murky water at the edge of the bog.

"Flaming fireballs!" I whispered. "It worked." As I spoke, a puff of smoke came out of my mouth. I was a real dragon — from my flared flame-coloured nostrils, right down to the tip of my gold-spiked tail.

"Bella?" I could hear Little Woo's tiny voice coming from somewhere above me. "Is that still you in there?"

"Yes!" I said, calling out to her. "Of course it's me. Where are you?" My roar was so loud that flames shot out of my jaws. "Ahhh!" I tried to blow a smoke ring instead, but it was too late. My fiery breath had caught the branches of the tree where Little Woo was hiding. She shot into the air with smoke streaming from her singed tail feathers and my precious wand in her claws.

"Sorry!" I whispered, trying to keep my voice as low as I could so that no more fire would shoot out of my mouth.

The whole tree had gone up in flames by now, like a giant bonfire. Little Woo was lucky to have escaped in time.

Even the endless rain didn't dampen my magic dragon flames as the fire took hold. I tried to blow on the crackling blaze to extinguish it myself. But that only made things worse. With one puff of my mighty breath, the red-hot tongues of fire were blown from the tree to the spiky thorn hedge as well.

POOF!

It was as if it had been hit with dynamite. It began to blaze and roar. Within seconds the whole hedge was a wall of fire.

"Scalding scorpions!" I cried. "What have I done?" That only made things worse, of course, as more flames shot out of my mouth. Being a fire-breathing dragon was much harder than I'd thought.

"Little Woo?" I whispered. "Where are you? Are you safe?"

"I'm fine." Her voice sounded wheezy as she called out to me through the smoke from somewhere high above my head. "Well done, Bella." She coughed. "You can burn the whole hedge down like that."

"You're right. Fly away and I'll join you as quick as I can," I whispered. "Keep out of the smoke." The hedge would be nothing more than a pile of ash in a few moments.

I could simply step over it and escape.

I watched as the flames licked the dry branches – the thorns turned bright red, like hot iron. I edged back, swishing my tail to clear the smoke and waited for the hedge to smoulder away to nothing.

But the flames just kept on dancing in the branches, Finally, I realized the giant thorn bush wasn't burning down at all. The magic hedge glowed red-hot but did not blacken or char like the tree had done. As each flame flickered away, another two shot up in its place. The whole hedge was a great glowing wall of fire, which showed no sign of burning itself out and seemed as if it could go on blazing like that for ever.

Yet again, I had made things worse. Instead of just thorns I would have fight my way over roaring flames now too.

"I'm coming, Little Woo," I whispered,

hoping she had already taken my wand with her and flown far away to safety on the other side. There was no point in putting it off. This is what I had wings for. If I wanted to escape from this horrible place, I would have to fly high above the blazing wall of flames and join her.

I took three big steps backwards, swishing my tail behind me as I went. Then I arched my back and flexed my shoulders.

Whoosh!

There was a sound like a hundred umbrellas opening as my huge red wings spread out beside me. I could see their tips from the corner of my eye, shimmering with silver and gold, so bright they glistened like jewels in thick smoke all around.

I flexed my shoulders again, flapped my wings just once, and felt my clawed feet lift off from the ground.

I flapped twice more and rose like an eagle. The moment I was airborne, my huge dragon's body felt as light as a feather.

Up, up, up into the smoky sky, I soared.

Chapter Seventeen

Flying felt wonderful!

With each flick of my mighty dragon's wings, I rose higher and higher into the sky.

In just a few wingbeats I would be up, over the hedge and away. The flaming thorn bushes crackled and roared beneath me.

"Careful, Bella!" hooted Little Woo, watching from the safety of a tall rock on the other side.

All I had to do was glide over the blazing

hedge and I'd be free to fly away and join her.

BOOM!

The minute I tried to cross the hedge, sparks shot into the air like fireworks.

"Ouch!" It wasn't just sparks that were flying, it was burning thorns too. Each one was as hot and sharp as a blazing arrow.

"Ouch!" I squealed again. Dragons have thick skin like leather armour all over their bodies... All over their bodies except under their soft bellies. The skin there is as thin as a velvet duster.

"Ouch! Ouch! Ouchhhhhhhhhhh!" I whimpered as the burning thorns pierced my tender undercarriage.

I coiled up like a shrimp, trying to protect my tummy, and toppled backwards through the sky.

Wham!

I landed with a shuddering thud on the stony ground back outside Aunt Hemlock's cave. The spell hadn't worked. I was still trapped on the wrong side of the thorny wall. "Splintering spooks!" I groaned as I lay still for a moment, gasping for breath like a giant scaly fish.

"Are you all right, Bella?" hooted Little Woo.

"Yes! Stay there," I warned her, trying to lift my head. The hedge was burning more wildly than ever.

But I wasn't going to be put off. Not yet. I staggered to my feet, unfurled my battered wings and tried again, this time flying even higher. But it was hopeless – I was thrown backwards by a great *WHOOSH* of hot air. My huge leathery body was tossed away by the boiling blast as if I wasn't a mighty dragon at all, but a tiny dragonfly in a breeze.

I had three more goes, getting faster and higher with every attempt, but it was still no good. Each time I was tossed backwards or attacked by blazing thorns until I landed in front of Aunt Hemlock's cave yet again with the wind knocked out of my huge fire-breathing lungs.

"I'll never escape from this place," I panted, staggering to my feet. "Aunt Hemlock's magic is just too strong."

I felt a hot burning feeling growing inside me. Not just flames this time, but anger too. Dragon anger.

I bellowed as my breath came back. It was so unfair of Aunt Hemlock to imprison me here like this. How dare she take me away from my wonderful foster parents who loved me so much? How dare she ruin my wonderful happy new life?

I don't know if it was the dragon in me, or just because I was so fed up, but I suddenly felt angrier than I had ever felt before. Of all the cruel things Aunt Hemlock had ever done to me, this was the cruellest yet. She had kidnapped me and shut me in behind this wall of thorns, all so that she could steal my tears to make her wicked potions.

"Well I won't stay here!" I roared, and blazing gasps of fire shot out of my mouth. "I won't stay here! And I will not cry!" The long scroll with all Aunt Hemlock's horrid tasks written on it burst into flames and turned to blackened ashes in an instant.

"Ha!" I roared as I swung round, my

huge tail sending her cauldron skittering across the ground so it bounced and dented on a rock.

"Bella?" said Little Woo, risking everything to fly back over the burning bushes and hover bravely above my head. "Bella, are you all right?"

"No!" I said. "I'm not all right. I am furious... Furious with Aunt Hemlock." And I thought of all the terrible things she had done to Little Woo too, stealing the new-hatched owlet from her parents' nest. "It's just not fair," I roared. Red and orange flames burst out of my jaws and fire streamed from my nostrils. Some of the flames shot out so far, they rushed right through the door of Aunt Hemlock's cave.

BOOM! CRACK! POP! BANG!

There was a sound like a million

fireworks all going off at once.

"The potions!" I cried. "They're exploding!"

Sparks shot out of the mouth of cave. Red, orange, yellow, green, blue, indigo, violet. Every colour of the rainbow – and gold, copper, bronze and silver too. There were stars, and swirls and spirals, all spinning in the air like crazy Catherine wheels on Bonfire Night.

Aunt Hemlock's store of potions had all gone BANG like a factory full of popping candy.

"I can't believe it! Everything will be ruined!" I cheered. It felt wonderful to know that all those dreadful potions couldn't hurt anybody now. I swished my mighty dragon tail with joy.

"The colours are so pretty," hooted Little Woo. "I've never seen anything so beautiful in all my life."

She was right. The sparks and spirals were beautiful. But there was a terrible stink in the air too – of toenails and gassy toad farts and fungus. I reeled back as a bubbling jar of pickled eyeballs, the charred remains of a mummy's finger and a smouldering newt skin shot through the air and landed at my feet.

As the final shower of sparkles fizzled away, my huge dragon knees began to shake. These weren't just pretty fireworks on a village green. This was Aunt Hemlock's precious potion collection going up in smoke . . . and the hot flames of my angry dragon's breath had caused it all.

"Spluttering spells," I whispered, as billowing clouds of green and purple smoke spewed out of the rocky doorway. "I've just exploded Aunt Hemlock's cave."

"And look," hooted Little Woo, swooping

in circles round and round my head. "Look, Bella. She's on her way back."

I glanced up through the thick clouds of stinking smoke. Far away on the horizon was the shadowy shape of a witch, a chameleon and a broomstick.

Aunt Hemlock was coming home.

Chapter Eighteen

As I looked at the horizon and saw Aunt Hemlock riding her broomstick towards us, an icy shiver ran down my spine – right to the tip of my long red tail. All the dragon anger inside me turned to fear. It was a wonderful thing to have blown up Aunt Hemlock's potion store – all those dreadful mixtures were useless now. They could never do anyone any harm. But Aunt Hemlock was not going to be pleased. Not one little bit.

"Gibbering jellyfish!" I quivered. "I'm in big trouble now."

The moment cold fear begin to twist inside me, something extraordinary happened. I felt the flames in my huge fiery dragon's heart flicker and fade. What had felt like a bright, burning coal in my chest was more like an anxious fluttering butterfly now.

POOF!

My thick scaly skin fell away like the peeling bark of a tree, and my flaming breath came out as nothing more than hollow gasps. Real dragons do not feel fear, I suppose. As soon as I let my worry about Aunt Hemlock in, my magic disguise vanished like a puff of smoke. Suddenly, there was no long red tail or golden claws – I was not a magnificent fire-breathing beast any more. I was just me again, ordinary Bella Broomstick, in my blue spotty pyjamas and yellow welly boots.

"Oh, Little Woo. What am I going to do?" I gasped, as she dropped my flamingo wand safely back into my hand. It was too late to try any fresh magic now. I stuffed the pen into my pocket as Aunt Hemlock's broomstick roared through the sky towards us. "How am I going to explain all this mess?"

A thick purple-green goo like bubbling lava was oozing out of the door of the cave where all the gassy potions had burst from their bottles in the heat of my dragon's flames.

"Poo!" Little Woo was too busy fanning her beak with her wings to answer. "Sorry." She choked. I couldn't blame her. The stench from the bubbling lava was horrific – like rotten eggs and troll breath and ogre feet all rolled into one enormous smelly swamp-monster burp.

"Puh!" We both began to cough and wheeze. Before either of us could catch our breath to speak again, Aunt Hemlock had swept over the smouldering ring of thorns and landed on the swampy ground beside me.

"So you're back, are you?" she said, looking at Little Woo. "Then she wrinkled her nose. "Hmm. What's that delicious smell...?"

"Delicious?" I spluttered. Trust Aunt Hemlock to think the stinking pong of belching gas was nice. I felt a ray of hope. Perhaps she wouldn't be angry with me after all. Perhaps she'd bottle the goo and sell it as a witch's perfume.

But as she turned her head and looked around, the smile faded from her lips. I saw her narrow eyes widen with horror as they took in the smoke-filled cave, the shards of broken glass and the bubbling goo spewing from her doorway.

"My potions! They're ruined," she roared, grabbing me by the scruff of my neck. "What have you done?"

"I – er – I. . ." It was no use. I couldn't have answered even if I'd had a good excuse. Aunt Hemlock was half-strangling me as she held me dangling in mid-air.

"There was a dragon!" hooted Little Woo, truthfully. "It was nothing to do with Bella." (That wasn't quite so truthful, of course.)

"A dragon?" Aunt Hemlock dropped me to the ground with a bump.

"Yes," said Little Woo. "A huge, big red one. And its hot steaming breath made everything go BANG!"

"That's right." I nodded my head. Whatever happened, I didn't want Aunt Hemlock to guess that I had actually turned myself into the fiery beast. She thought she'd confiscated my wand when she took the little windup torch away. As long as she believed that, she'd think that I couldn't do any magic without it. The secret of my flamingo pen would be safe.

I slipped my fingers into my coat pocket and felt the soft feathers hidden away from view.

"It was all because of number eighty-three on your list of chores," I said. "You know, the one about getting hair from a dragon's nostril." Again, that was half-true, at least. It was seeing the terrifying task on the bottom of the list which had given me the idea to turn myself into a dragon in the first place.

"I see!" Aunt Hemlock towered over me. Wane was perched on her shoulder, staring down at me too as he licked his thin, blue chameleon lips.

"Oh dear!" He smirked. "You've done it this time, Belladonna."

"Let me get this straight," said Aunt Hemlock slowly, "you called a dragon here ... right up close to the cave, just so that you could take a single hair from its nostril?"

"Well, not exactly," I stammered. "Now you put it like that..." I could see that the story wasn't such a clever one after all. Perhaps I should just say that a dragon came here of its own accord.

But it was too late. Little Woo was jumping up and down, hooting in outrage as she leapt to my defence.

"Of course Bella called the dragon," she said. "How else was she supposed to find one? She wasn't allowed to go beyond the ring of thorns."

"Silence!" growled Aunt Hemlock.

But Little Woo bravely carried on – fibbing her feathers off as she tried to help me out.

"Bella was amazing," she hooted. "She roared for the fiery dragon in its own language and it came flying across the sky, all the way from the far mountains. She's so clever, you know."

"Clever?" Aunt Hemlock threw her arms in the air so her cloak spread out like the giant black wings of a vampire bat. "Belladonna isn't clever. She is a fool... The most hopeless young witch I have ever met."

"Hopeless!" agreed Wane.

"Who else except a soppy animal-loving idiot like Belladonna would call a dragon to come right up close to their home?" Aunt Hemlock snarled.

"But this cave isn't my home," I muttered under my breath. "My home is at Honeysuckle Cottage."

Aunt Hemlock either didn't hear or didn't care.

"Soft-witted fool!" she roared.

"Fool!" agreed Wane.

Aunt Hemlock marched up to the door of her cave and stared into the billowing smoke.

"Come here!" she bellowed, clicking her fingers at me. "I can't even see my own nose! Make this thing of yours shine." She held out the little windup froggy-torch that she was so sure was my wand. "Go on! If you're so clever, do a spell." She thrust it into my hand. "Make me some magic light so I can see the damage you have caused."

"All right..." I swished the torch from side to side a little and murmured something under my breath which I hoped sounded like a bit like a spell.

Blah blah blah, bring some light
Blah blah blah, shining bright.

I squeezed my shaking fingers around the plastic frog's legs, pumping the torch into life as light flooded the smoky cave.

"Twisting tornadoes!" I gasped as I saw the terrible mess inside. The grey fungus-covered walls were scorched soot-black. The floor was covered with broken glass and bubbling goo. The wooden potion shelves had burnt away like log on a fire.

Not a single jar, bottle or pot stood upright any more. Everything had exploded in the flames.

"My beautiful, precious potions are all ruined!" Aunt Hemlock screamed. "All of them! How am I supposed to give my enemies a dose of itchy warts now? Or send a rival raving mad with my best Worry Lotion? Where will I find the powders to make a fog so thick that those who cross me will be lost in it for ever?"

"I ... I don't know," I said quietly.

"You will pay for this, Belladonna." Aunt Hemlock pointed her thin, white wand straight at my heart.

"Please," I begged. But she was already muttering her spell.

POOF!

I felt as if I had been punched in the chest as the smoky cave filled with angry sparks of dark green magic.

My knees buckled beneath me. The little froggy torch fell from my hand. I sank down to the ground. Down, down, down – melting into a small, sticky mess.

Chapter Nineteen

"Bella?"

I could hear Little Woo hooting for me.

"Bella. Where are you?"

"Here," I called out to her as loudly as I could. "I'm down here."

"Where?" Little Woo landed in the entrance to Aunt Hemlock's cave and looked around her.

"Careful!" I cried in a squelchy voice. She almost trod on me, I was so small.

"Bella!" she gasped as she spotted me at last. "You're a. . ."

"A slug! Yes," I said with a soggy sigh. I didn't need to look in a mirror to know it was true. The soft gloopy feeling in my body was all too familiar from the many times Aunt Hemlock had punished me like this before. If I did need proof, my eyes were now on the end of two long stalks poking out the top of my head. I could swivel them round and see all the way along my squishy, legless body to the tip of my slippery slug tail if I wanted to.

"What are you going to do?" whispered Little Woo.

Aunt Hemlock and Wane had vanished deep inside the smoky cave to examine the damage my fiery dragon's breath had caused.

"I don't know," I groaned as I crawled slowly outside into the pale sunlight, squelching as I went. A familiar cold sadness was growing inside me. That's the worst thing about being a slug. It's not that you can't run or jump, or that sharp stones dig into your soft belly every time you move. It's not that you never get to eat anything except soggy leaves. It's not even the endless trails of sticky goo you have to sit in all the time. The worst thing about being a slug is the dull, damp feeling of misery. Like you'll never really care about anything ever again.

"What does it matter?" I said. "What does anything matter? I'll just stay here like this until Aunt Hemlock decides to turn me back again. Then she can steal my tears and keep me here for ever." There was nothing else I could do. I couldn't use my wand. It had been in my pocket when Aunt Hemlock cast her spell. My whole coat and everything inside it was all part of my thick rubbery slug skin now. I knew I would never get my magical flamingo pen back until the curse was lifted and I was turned back into a girl. There didn't seem to be much chance of that.

"I don't really care what happens to me any more," I said with a little wet shiver.

"Yes you do!" cried Little Woo. "You care lots and lots, Bella." She bent down so close to me with her sharp beak that I thought she might be going to eat me.

"Go ahead," I said dully. "At least I might make you a nice snack."

But Little Woo did not want to eat me. Instead, she gently pressed her beak against the side of my soggy head. I think it was a sort of kiss or a hug. It's hard to tell when you're a slug ... but I felt the warmth and friendship rush through me like a sip of warm tea on a cold day.

"I care what happens to you, Bella!" said Little Woo. "And you care, too. You care because you want to get back to your family. To your uncle Martin and aunty Rose. And to Rascal, the little kitten you told me about."

"You're right." I blinked as a single sluggy tear fell from the corner of my eye and rolled all the way down the long stalk to plop on to my head. I froze for a moment, half expecting Aunt Hemlock to appear with her collecting jar. But I could still hear her bellowing with rage inside the cave.

"I do care, Woo," I whispered. Somewhere

deep inside my cold, rubbery skin, I felt a warm glow. I tried to stay focused on that – like a tiny beating heart inside me. I thought about Aunty Rose and Uncle Martin and Rascal too.

"I can still find my way home to them," I said. "Even if I'm nothing but a slug. Even if I don't have my wand. I can still do it!"

"Of course you can!" cheered Little Woo.

I slithered forward, leaving a sticky slug trail behind me. It's an odd feeling, moving around as a slug – like rolling in glue when you've just got out the bath. But, at last, I reached the high thorn hedge.

Little Woo followed.

"Look," I said as she landed on the ground beside me. "I think there might be a way through." My eyeballs quivered on the end of their stalks. The hedge was far too tall for me to see over it, of course.

But lying flat on my belly down here by the roots, I could see a criss-cross of little pathways winding their way beneath the spiky branches. Down in the darkness, I could see tiny ants and beetles scurrying along the miniature footpaths, finding a way out under the hedge.

"If they can do it, so can I," I whispered. I could even see a pale glimmer of grey daylight on the other side. "I couldn't fly over when I was a mighty dragon, but perhaps I can crawl under now I'm a tiny slug."

"But won't the magic stop you?" asked Little Woo, suddenly sounding worried again.

"I'm not sure," I said, hoping I was so small and low to the ground I could secretly slither through unnoticed. "There's only one way to find out."

I held my breath and edged forward, following a scuttling spider along a tiny twisting track.

"YOW!" I only had taken three sluggy wriggles when the thorns began to rain down on me from above. "Prickly pin cushions," I cried as I turned around in a sticky circle and retreated back to where I had come from. "It's no good. I'll never get through."

There where so many thorns sticking into me, I looked more like a mini porcupine than a slug.

"You poor thing," cooed Little Woo as she gently pulled each spike out for me with her beak.

A little way off, I could hear Aunt Hemlock cursing as she clattered about amongst the broken potion bottles and jars in her cave.

"Belladonna Broomstick can spend the

rest of her life as a slug for all I care," she wailed. "Even her tears are useless now she has destroyed all the other ingredients in my potion store."

"Quite right!" agreed Wane. "You might as well just boil her up and make slug jam."

"That's not a bad idea," Aunt Hemlock cackled and I slid behind a patch of nettles to hide.

An endless grey drizzle was beating down as usual.

"I'll never ever escape from this place," I murmured as all of my sad, soggy slug feelings returned. The hedge of thorns was just too clever for me. No matter what I tried, there was no way to get through it.

I was cold and tired and bruised all over. Even the thought that I had prevented all those hideous new potions from being brewed couldn't cheer me up. I realized that the last time I had slept was the few hours I had managed to nap back in the tent with Uncle Martin and Aunty Rose. My eyes felt heavy and stalks on the top of my head began to droop.

Little Woo perched in a crooked tree above me and dozed with one eye open as if she was keeping guard.

"Sweet dreams," I whispered sleepily.

That seemed the most that either of us could hope for now.

Chapter Twenty

"Twit-woo. Twit-woo."

Little Woo's frightened voice woke me. It was dark. The strange green full moon had risen high over the Magic Realm ... and it was still raining, of course.

"What is it? What's the matter, Little Woo?" I yawned and wriggled a bit, trying to stretch my arms and legs, before I remembered I didn't have any. I was still a slug.

"Sorry, Bella. I didn't mean to wake you,"

said Little Woo, but she began chattering away at once. "It's just that I was out here all on my own . . . and it's very dark. You've been asleep for hours, you know."

"Have I?" I murmured, wishing I could roll over and go straight back to sleep. But that's the trouble with being friends with an owl. She wanted to talk all night.

"I thought you'd never wake up," she said, her voice shaking a little. "There've been so many strange sounds. Mumbles and grumbles and rumbles."

"Oh dear. Poor you," I said, realizing she really was afraid of the dark. The Magic Realm was full of horrible sounds at night. I could hear the howl of a werewolf somewhere in the woods and the screech of a vampire bat hunting on the marsh. Closer to us, there was a different sort of noise, but it still sent a shiver through me as I heard Aunt Hemlock's snores coming from the cave and Wane's dry raspy breaths as he slept too. It reminded me that I was still a prisoner in this awful place.

"Tell me something cheerful – if you can still manage that while you're a slug," said Little Woo, flying down to the ground to perch beside me on a stone. "Tell me again about Honeysuckle Cottage. Tell me everything you can remember. Tell me what you used to eat."

So, as my poor sluggy tummy rumbled, I told Little Woo about all the things I liked best... "There's Chinese takeaway, of course. And doughnuts and pancakes and roast dinners and spaghetti bolognese.

Ice cream and blueberry muffins and hot buttered toast and... Please, Little Woo," I cried. "Don't make me tell you any more. I think I'm going to explode with hunger." I chewed on a bitter stinging nettle leaf, which is the sort of thing slugs like, I suppose. But it didn't make me feel any better. The thought that I'd never taste Aunty Rose's home-made chocolate cake ever again was too much to bear.

"Tell me about your house, then," said Little Woo.

So I began to describe the pretty thatched cottage and the lovely garden too. It was funny, but talking about it actually did make me feel better. I told her all about the special owl nesting box Uncle Martin and I had put up in the old oak tree.

"Any owls in the Person World who want to can come and nest there," I explained. "You'd love it, Little Woo. I painted it in rainbow colours, and magic stars sparkle on the roof. It's high up in the branches, right at the bottom of the garden."

"It does sound lovely," she hooted.

"It is! Everything about Honeysuckle Cottage is just perfect," I said, feeling a pale flicker of warmth glowing deep inside my cold sluggy body again. "Even if I never get to go back there, I'll always have my memories at least."

"You're lucky," said Little Woo. "I wish I could remember more about my nest, then maybe I could find my way home."

"Oh, Woo!" I said, wishing I could reach over and hug her – but nobody wants a sticky wet hug from a slug. "If only there was something I could do to help you get back to your family."

"I know you'd help if could, Bella." Little Woo blinked and her big golden eyes looked pale and sad in the moonlight. "But there is nothing you can do, is there? You're a slug . . . and you're stuck here on the wrong side of the wall of thorns."

"I promised I'd help you find your family when we first met," I said. "And I still will, if I ever get the chance."

"You don't have to stick to it. It wasn't a real promise," said Little Woo. She made a sad little sound halfway between a hoot and sniff. "I tricked you, remember – all because your stinky old aunt knew you would offer to help and she could lure you back to the Magic Realm if you did."

"No, Little Woo," I said, remembering what Aunty Rose and Uncle Martin had said about how strong and important promises are. "A promise is a promise!" I assured her, and a tiny smile tickled the corner of my sluggy mouth. "Dancing dragonflies," I cried. "I think I've got a plan! I may know a way to get out of here, after all."

"How?" said Little Woo miserably. "You've tried everything you can to get through the hedge of thorns. It's hopeless. You said so yourself. You don't even have a wand any more ... not since it was inside your pocket when Aunt Hemlock cast her horrible spell. Your whole coat is part of your slug skin now. You won't get your magic pen back unless you turn into a girl."

She looked down at me and shook her head in pity.

I swallowed hard, trying not to think too much about my wonderful enchanted pen. Or what would happen if I never got it back at all.

"I know I don't have a wand any more,"
I said. "But we won't need magic. Or not
like that. Not a spell."

"Oh?" Little Woo ruffled her feathers.

"I promised I would help you find your
family and that's what I am going to do,"
I said.

I listened for a moment to make sure
that I could still hear the sound of Aunt
Hemlock and Wane safely snoring in the
cave. Then I slid across the moonlit ground
towards the towering thorn hedge.

"Do you think you could carry me in
your beak, Little Woo?" I asked.

"Of course," she said. "You're only a tiny
slug, after all."

"Good!" I slithered
towards her as Little
Woo opened her beak
and very gently lifted

me off the ground.

"Eeek!" I squealed. "That tickles!"

"Sorr—" Little Woo began to apologize. But I stopped her just in time.

"Don't speak!" I warned her. "Or you'll drop me. Now hold tight and fly over the hedge if you can."

I looked up past her beak saw the look of panic in Little Woo's eyes. I knew what she was thinking. The magic hedge would attack me again. Thorns would fly through the air like arrows just as they had every time I had tried to pass over or under it before.

"It'll be different," I told her. A nervous shiver ran through me and I hoped I was right. "Until now, I've been trying to use spells to force my way through to the other side ... when all I needed to do was remember that I had made a solemn promise to help somebody else."

I knew Little Woo didn't really understand what I was saying, but she seemed to trust me all the same. She gave a gentle nod and flapped her wings. A moment later we were in the air.

All this time, I'd been trying to get myself home. But that was a selfish wish. It was never going to break down the wall of thorns... Not before I had honoured my promise to Little Woo. What was it Aunty Rose and Uncle Martin had said? "A promise is a very powerful thing – stronger than an iron bar or the bricks which built Honeysuckle Cottage." Perhaps a promise was even more powerful than Aunt Hemlock's wicked magic, too.

I took a deep breath – or as deep as I could manage with Little Woo's beak pressed around my sluggy tummy. Then I began to chant. It wasn't a spell exactly – there was no point without my wand. But it was a reminder that I had given my word of honour to help the little owl get home...

> Oh, *Wall of Thorns, let me pass through,*
> *I pledged to help poor Little Woo.*
> *I need to find her family now,*
> *You cannot halt my solemn vow.*

I looked down and saw that we were high above the hedge already.

"Glistening glow-worms!" I gasped in disbelief as every angry thorn below us turned into a yellow rose. Instead of sharp spikes, soft petals were shimmering in the moonlight.

"We've done it, Little Woo," I cried as we soared through the sky and away across the marsh. "We're free!"

Chapter Twenty-One

"Well done, Little Woo!" I cried as we flew through the sky. "Head for the woods and let's see if we can find your nest."

I couldn't believe it. My little sluggy eyes were practically popping off the end of their stalks as I looked behind us and saw that we really had escaped from Aunty Hemlock's thorny prison at last. The prickly hedge that had held me back for so long was covered in hundreds of pretty golden blooms. The scent of roses filled the chilly air and even the rain had left off.

"We did it!" I cheered.

But the moment I spoke, there was a whooshing sound and a puff of green smoke as a broomstick shot up into the air behind us.

"Aunt Hemlock!" I gasped. She must have woken up. And now she knew I was trying to escape.

"Bella Broomstick!" she roared. "Just where do you think you're going with that silly little owl?"

"We can see you in her beak, Sluggy. You can't escape us!" chuckled Wane.

"Stop, Owl!" Aunt Hemlock bellowed, raising her wand in the air. "Bring that slug-child back here. Right now."

"Fly on! Ignore them, Little Woo." I begged.

But the poor, frightened owl seemed almost frozen in mid-air.

"Oh dear! Oh dear!" she flustered and began to fly in circles round and round.

"Go on!" I urged. "Or Aunt Hemlock will get us both."

But Aunt Hemlock seemed to be having problems of her own. Every time she tried to cross the wall of flowering roses she seemed to stop and shiver in mid-air.

"Achoo!" she sneezed and her broomstick bucked beneath like a wild horse. Her wand flew out of her hand and landed in the bog below.

"She can't cross over!" I cried. "Look, Little Woo! It's the roses. I think she's allergic!" I always knew Aunt Hemlock hated flowers. Now I saw why.

"Disgusting things," she squealed. "They

smell of hope and promises. Yuck! Yuck! Yuck!"

"Mistress," cried Wane, sneezing too. "Be careful."

As Little Woo circled helplessly round and round, I could see that the wobbly green warts on the end of Aunt Hemlock's nose were swelling to an enormous size. One was as big as a tennis ball.

"Achoo! Achoo! Fetch, my anti-loveliness spray, Wane!" she screamed. "I can't stand all this prettiness in one go. These roses stink of friendship and promises that have been kept!"

"But, Mistress," cried Wane. "There is no spray left. It all exploded when that foolish girl let the dragon into your potion store."

"Belladonna!" roared Aunt Hemlock, shaking her fist at me in the sky. "I'll get for you this!" One of her warts was as big as a football now.

"Achoo! Achoo! Achoo!" She sneezed so hard, she fell right off the broomstick and was left clinging on by one hand.

"A-a-a-a-choo!" echoed Wane, falling too so that he had to grab on to the broomstick with his tail.

All the while, they still couldn't cross the wall of roses.

"Fly on, Little Woo," I cried. "Don't you see? They can't get us. We're safe." And at last she seemed to find fresh courage. She beat her wings and we stopped circling and shot forward.

"Go, then!" growled Aunt Hemlock. "Achoo! See if I care. I don't want you here anyway."

"Good riddance, Belladonna Broomstick," wheezed Wane.

"You always were a hopeless witch . . . and now you've exploded my precious potion store," yelled Aunt Hemlock. "I'll never forgive you for that. Achoo! Achoo! It'll be years before I can make a decent new Misery Mist, or a Lotion of Woe, or even the tiniest Tincture of Despair," she wailed.

"Good! Even the Magic Realm might be a happier place without your wicked potions," I cried.

"Achoo!" Aunt Hemlock sneezed with violent rage, and finally fell off her broomstick, spinning through the air until

she landed head first in her cauldron with a *clang*!

"Yikes!" squealed Wane as the broom spun off like a firecracker and he fell through the air behind her.

"Come on, Little Woo. Let's go," I cried. I didn't even swivel my stalky eyes to look back as we swooped away across the marsh.

"We've done it," I said as she flew on towards the dark woods on the horizon. "We've escaped. Aunt Hemlock will be stuck behind that hedge for a good while yet. I can help you find your nest and then … and then…" I barely dared to hope. "Then perhaps I can go home too," I whispered.

I felt such a surge of joy that it was like a lightning bolt passing through me.

"Whirling weasels!" I cried. My whole sluggy body seemed to fizz as if I had been dipped in a bucket of sherbet. All the dull, damp sadness I had felt was gone.

Swirling excitement filled me now.

"Bella!" Little Woo gasped, opening her beak. "I can't hold you..."

"I know!" I screamed. "It's not your fault."

I was already falling towards the ground ... tumbling over and over in somersaults. I caught sight of my hands ... then my knees ... then my feet in yellow wellington boots.

No wonder Little Woo couldn't hold me. I wasn't a slug any more – I was a girl.

"I'm me!" I cheered. "I'm Bella Broomstick again!"

It was my excitement that had done it – all that hope and happiness had burst out of me like fireworks and transformed me back into my old self.

"Look out!" cried Little Woo. "You're going to crash!"

She was right.

"Help!" I screamed.

I was falling faster and faster towards the ground.

Chapter Twenty-Two

I was falling through the sky face first, my

arms spread out beside me like the wings of a bat.

For a moment I thought it might be all right. It was marshland below us after all — surely the soft ground would break my fall.

But as I saw the bubbling pools of mud and smelt the gassy air, I knew that if I hit the bog, the oozy mire might suck me straight under. I could drown in the horrible marshy goo.

Quick as a flash, I dug into my pocket and grabbed my wand, almost dropping it as I fell.

"Turn yourself back into a slug! I'll catch you," cried Little Woo.

But I had a better idea. I didn't want to be a slug again. Not ever, if I could help it. Out of the corner of my eye, I spotted a huge fallen tree, lying on its side in the marsh.

Waving my wand wildly, I yelled out at the top of my voice.

> *Don't let me fall in the soggy bog,*
> *Make me a broomstick from*
>   *that . . . log!*

Whoosh!

With a mighty belching sound like a troll's burp, the fallen tree shot up out of the swamp and soared into the air.

As it rose towards me, I managed to grab hold of a piece of rotten bark and fling my leg over the trunk, just a moment before I hit the boggy ground below.

"Diving demons! That was a close one." A second later and I'd have been swallowed up like a penny falling in a well. My breath was coming out in great gasps. I swallowed hard and steadied myself on the tree trunk with one hand. With the other, I waved my wand again, muttering the ancient broomstick-flying spell which every witch in Magic Realm knows by heart.

Sweep like wings into the sky,
Brush the clouds and fly, fly, fly!

I wasn't sure the spell would work. The old dead tree I was riding was hardly a real broomstick – it was as fat and round as a barrel ... and very, very soggy. Not to mention the little broken branches everywhere that were digging into me through my pyjamas as I clung on.

But to my relief, the huge trunk whooshed upwards, climbing through the sky like the pictures I've seen in the Person World of jumbo jets talking off.

I smiled as I remembered how jealous I had been of Piers going on an aeroplane for his holiday. "Fasten your seat belt, Little Woo. We're going for a ride!" I cried, tapping the trunk just behind me so that she could perch there and rest her tired wings. "We're going to find your nest and get you home at last."

The big tree trunk was not the most

graceful or elegant broomstick I had ever ridden, but it did the job. Before long, we had left the boggy marshland far behind and were flying above the deep, dark woods of the Magic Realm.

"This seems like a good place to start," I called over my shoulder to Little Woo. "You told me your nest was in a hollow tree."

"But that's all I remember," she hooted. "There are hundreds of trees in this wood. It could be any one of them."

"Yes," I said. "But we've got magic to help us now."

I raised my wand again.

Show us a sign so we may know
Which way to fly, which way to go.

At first there was nothing. Just the eerie green light of the moon above the dark trees, the moan of the wind and a fresh cold shower of rain which went right down the back on my neck.

Then suddenly there was a roar of thunder and a flash of lightening.

"Oh no!" I groaned. "A storm. That's all we need."

But for a moment, a bright fork of lightening hung in the air, just above a clearing in the trees. It was like an arrow pointing downwards...

"There!" I cried. And I tapped the side of my enormous flying broomstick with my wand. "Go left and land."

BOOM! BANG! CRASH!

If flying on the huge tree trunk was tricky, landing was even harder ... and not at all elegant, I'm afraid.

We smashed through the treetops, snapping off branches as we plunged towards the forest floor. Little Woo leapt off halfway down.

"Twit-woo! Twit-woo!" she cried in terror. "Be careful, Bella."

"I'm all right," I called, lifting my feet just in time as the flying trunk juddered to a halt, landing in a patch of undergrowth with a bone-rattling *thud*.

As I climbed down with shaky legs, I heard another voice answer Little Woo.

"Twit-woo! Twit-woo!"

And then another.

"Little Woo? Little Woo? Oh, my darling.

Is that you?"

"Mama?" Little Woo circled around the clearing. "Papa?"

Two speckled brown owl heads appeared from a hole in a hollow tree trunk above her.

"Little Woo!" they hooted. "We heard your voice. Oh, Little Woo, you've come home."

"I told you they'd never forget you," I whispered, as two younger owls flew out to join them.

They must be Little Woo's brother and sister.

As the five owls all hooted for joy, I clapped my hands and cheered.

I had kept my promise. Little Woo had found her family again at long last.

Now all I needed to do was find a way to get home to mine.

Chapter Twenty-Three

"Oh, Bella, are you sure you won't stay?" said Mama Owl.

Now that they had been reunited with their lost chick, the whole owl family were sitting in a line on a low branch above my head. Mama and Papa Owl had Little Woo between them, gently grooming her wings with

237

their beaks, while her big brother and sister hooted loudly at her from either end of the row.

"Tell us about the witch again, Woo?" screeched Twitty, her sister.

"Did she try to cook you in her cauldron?" asked her brother, Hooton.

"Shh!" said Mama Owl firmly. "I'm trying to talk to Bella.

"Yes, Bella. Please do stay," said Papa Owl. "You must be very hungry." He swivelled his head around to look in the direction of their hollow tree. "I think I've got a nice fat rat's tail left over, if you fancy that..."

"Er – no thank you," I said quickly. He looked a little offended. "It's very kind of you to offer," I explained. "But I really do have to be going." It was nearly dawn. I didn't want Aunt Hemlock to change her mind and come looking for me if she ever found a way to break through the wall of roses. "I need to get back to my family too, you see."

"Of course, of course!" hooted Mama Owl. "We won't hold you up for a moment longer."

"How about a rat's tail to take with you?" asked Papa Owl.

"No, thank you." I shook my head firmly. Even though I hadn't eaten a proper meal since I arrived in the Magic Realm, I wasn't hungry enough to try a rat's tail yet. My tummy rumbled all the same. "I'm sure my aunty and uncle will make something for me as soon I arrive," I said, almost drooling at the thought of a delicious breakfast cooked on the camp stove.

"We can never thank you enough for bringing our Little Woo home to us," said Mama Owl.

"Quite so. Quite so," hooted Papa Owl. "We thought we might never see her again."

"Thank you, Bella," said Twitty and Hooton. "Thank you! Thank you! Twit-woo. Twit-woo."

"Come on! Back to the nest with you two now." Mama Owl flapped her wings at them. "I'm sure Bella and Little Woo would like a moment's peace to say goodbye."

"It was lovely to meet you all," I said as Little Woo swooped down on to my shoulder and nibbled my ear.

"I'll never forget you, Bella," she said.

"And I'll never forget you either, Little Woo." I stroked her feathery head one last time, then she flew up to a branch above her nest hole in the hollow tree. The whole owl family poked their heads out once again and hooted, "Goodbye."

"Goodbye," I said, swallowing hard. I wasn't going to let myself cry – not yet. Not while I was still in the Magic Realm. But my hands were shaking as I clambered back on board my tree trunk broomstick and raised my wand.

Sweep like wings into the sky,
Brush the clouds and fly, fly, fly!

The huge broom wobbled and rose up with a groan.

"How are you going to get back to the Person World?" hooted Little Woo.

"Don't worry," I said as the giant log reared up like a knight's charger. "This broomstick is big enough to break through anything – even the Curtain of Invisibility ... if I can find it."

"I think we may be able to help you

there," said Mama Owl, poking her head out of the nest again. "We've often flown into something cold and wet when we're hunting at night. Could that be what you are looking for?"

"It's like being hit in the face with a dead fish," added Papa Owl, poking his head out beside her.

"That's it!" I cried. "That's exactly it."

"Fly on towards the rising sun. Fast and straight and you can't miss it," said Mama Owl.

"Thank you! Goodbye to you all," I called over my shoulder as my enormous broomstick crashed through the tree tops and up into the dawn sky. I leant forward and tapped my wand three times on the trunk.

Find that curtain now, dear tree,
Take me through and set me free.

The huge log hurtled away across the sky.

"Giddy-up!" I giggled, certain that with a little magic and the advice of the wise owls, my funny broomstick would get me home at last.

Sure enough, when we had left the wood far behind and flown on through the wind and rain; all across the marshland, I recognized the place where I'd first come through to the Magic Realm with Little Woo. I plunged on, straight as an arrow, and suddenly felt a cold, wet slap in the face.

"The Curtain of Invisibility!" I cheered as I flew out of the grey clouds into a warm flood of bright early morning sunlight. It was a beautiful spring day, the sun was shining and I was back in the Person World at last.

Flying high above the trees, I spotted our little red car far below – just as it was when I'd left – still stuck in the mud on the track through the woods.

I tapped my wand three times on my flying tree trunk and held my breath as it crashed down to the ground, almost blocking the track behind the car as it landed with a heavy *thud*. I leapt off and looked around me, making sure that no one had seen me in the quiet woods. It would be hard enough to explain why I was flying a broomstick in the Person World, let alone a whole tree trunk.

But the only one who had noticed was a curious wood mouse.

"What a wonderful old tree," she chirped in a tiny voice, sniffing at the trunk as she crept forward. "Is it yours?"

"Er – not any more," I said. "I don't think I'll need it now."

"Perfect!" said the mouse. "I was looking for a new house... And it's so spacious."

"Then you're welcome to it," I said, delighted that old tree could make someone so happy. "Goodbye. I hope you enjoy your new home."

I began to run along the path. But, just before I put my wand away, I turned and cast one last tiny spell.

Set our car wheels free from goo
So we can go home . . . when we're ready to.

I stuffed the flamingo pen deep into my pocket and charged helter-skelter through the trees to where I could see our little blue tent, still safely standing in the middle of the clearing.

"Aunty Rose!" I cried. "Uncle Martin! Are you there?"

"Of course we're here!" Two smiling faces popped out of the end of the tent.

I had to laugh – they looked just like

Mama and Papa Owl, poking their heads out of the nest hole in their hollow tree. But at least I knew the spell I had cast on them before I left had worked. I could tell at once they hadn't been worried or missed me at all while I was gone.

"You're up early, Bella," said Aunty Rose brightly. "Have you been exploring the woods?"

"Sort of," I said, and I flung my arms around them both, almost knocking the tent to the ground in my excitement at finally being with them once again.

"Steady on!" chuckled Uncle Martin.

"Sorry! I'm just glad to be back, that's all," I said, and my eyes filled up with tears.

"You've only been for a little walk." Aunty Rose looked at me strangely.

I turned quickly away, wiping the precious tears with the edge of my sleeve. I smiled to myself as I thought how much Aunt Hemlock would love to fill her horrid jar with those. Then I turned around again, grinning from ear to ear.

"Are you ready for breakfast?" asked Aunty Rose gently.

"How about a nice big fry-up?" suggested Uncle Martin.

"Yum! That would be perfect," I said and

my tummy rumbled like a growling ogre.

"Sounds like I'd better get a move on!" Uncle Martin chuckled.

"There's no hurry," I said. And it was true. I'd have the whole of the rest of the week to spend with them at the campsite now. After that, we could all go home together to Honeysuckle Cottage (and order Chinese takeaway for supper if I was lucky!).

Life would return to normal at long last.

Chapter Twenty-four

Camping was wonderful. It was the first holiday I had ever been on in my whole life. I didn't care that there was no fancy hotel with a pool, or that we hadn't flown away on an aeroplane like Piers and his family. I was just happy to be with Uncle Martin and Aunty Rose – playing card games, going for long muddy walks, and eating our dinner under the stars. And it only rained twice. The one thing I was sad about was that the little froggy torch was lost for ever.

"Don't worry," said Uncle Martin when I told him I didn't have it any more. "It might turn up when we pack everything away."

I knew it wouldn't, of course. It had been left behind in the Magic Realm – Aunt Hemlock was probably still trying to figure out how to get it to work. I wondered if she was still stuck behind the wall of roses too. But I shook my head and tried not to think about it too much. She had said she never wanted to see me again after I had ruined her precious potion store, and I was willing to believe that. Destroying those dreadful mixtures was a wonderful thing to have done. Life for everyone (except Aunt Hemlock herself) would be far better without them. I smiled as I thought of Little

Woo back with her gorgeous family . . . and I was here with mine. I was safe and happy again at last. I was on holiday without a care in the whole wide Person World.

Yet all too soon, it was time to pack up and leave the woods. Even though I'd had such a brilliant week camping, a big part of me was pleased to be going home. The holiday had been really fun, but I couldn't quite remember now why I had ever been so desperate to go away. I was longing to see Honeysuckle Cottage again – the best place that there was. I couldn't wait to see Rascal too, and give him a great big squishy hug.

I needn't have bothered. He was in a very bad mood when we arrived.

"Mrs Brimblecombe from the post office has only ever looked after budgerigars before," he said, stalking off to sit on my bedroom windowsill with his back to me.

"She didn't know anything about cats. She never scratched me behind the ears like you do. All she fed me was a bowl of seeds and a dried cuttlefish."

"Nonsense! I saw an enormous pile of cat food tins in the recycling bin. Twice as many as you'd normally get through," I said, sitting down beside him and giving his ears an extra-long scratch.

"Humph!" said Rascal. "The only good news is that no pesky owls have come to live in that silly nest of yours yet." He narrowed his eyes and stared out of the window at the rainbow-coloured box Uncle Martin and I had hung in the old oak tree.

But later that night – after a delicious Chinese takeaway for supper – when I was I tucked up safely in my own little bed again at last, I heard a hoot echoing through the night sky.

"Bella Broomstick!" It called. "Bella Broomstick, are you there?"

I pelted down the stairs and out into the moonlit garden without even bothering to put on my dressing gown and slippers. As I stared up at our big old oak tree, I saw five little owls all in a row – Mama, Papa, Twitty, Hooton ... and, of course, Little Woo.

"Oh, Bella. There you are," she said, swooping down and landing on my shoulder. "I knew this was Honeysuckle Cottage the moment we flew over. I'd have recognized it anywhere — and then there was the rainbow nest box. I saw the stars twinkling on the roof from miles away."

"But what are you doing here?" I gasped. "I thought you were safe in your hollow tree in the Magic Realm."

"We were," said Papa Owl. "But Little Woo kept telling us all the things you had said about the Person World."

"It sounded so lovely," said Mama Owl.

"I wanted to see it for myself," said Hooton.

"And me," said Twitty.

"And me most of all!" hooted Little Woo.

"Oh! I am so glad you came," I said. "But how did you find your way?"

"Easy," said Little Woo. "Mama and Papa

already knew how to find the Curtain of Invisibility, so we flew straight through it.

"It was funny," moaned Twitty. "All cold and damp."

"Like being hit in the beak with a wet fish!" Hooton shuddered.

"Exactly," agreed Little Woo. "We knew we had made it to the Person World, then. We asked all the bats and birds and flying insects if any of them could tell us the way to Merrymeet Village."

"Everyone was so helpful and kind," said Mama Owl.

"All except a big iron bird who just roared at us," said Hooton.

"I expect that was an aeroplane!" I giggled.

"But a nice young robin showed us right to the edge of the village," said Twitty.

"And I spotted the stars twinkling on

your owl box straight away," said Little Woo. "Just like you told me, Bella."

"And now here we are," said Papa Owl.

"In your beautiful garden," said Mama Owl.

"And you're very welcome!" I told them. Although Rascal, who had just poked his head out of the door, hissed something extremely rude about "feather-brained birds" and stalked out into the darkness in a huff.

"We were wondering," said Little Woo shyly. "Could we perhaps ... I mean, would it be possible to... Do you think we could..."

"Stay here and live in the owl box?" I asked, guessing she might be too shy to ask.

"Yes," said Little Woo. "Could we?"

"Of course," I beamed. "Nothing would make me happier. Our rainbow nest box is perfect for you — it's just waiting to be home to a whole family of little owls."

"Twit-woo! Twit-woo!" They all hooted at once — so loudly that Uncle Martin poked his head out of his bedroom window.

"Bella?" he whispered. "Is that you down there? What are you doing in the garden at this time of night? I thought I heard an owl."

"Actually, Uncle Martin," I said innocently. "It wasn't one owl you heard . . . it was five of them. And I think they want to come and live in our nesting box."

"Really?" Uncle Martin was down the stairs quicker than a witch on a broomstick, almost tripping over Rascal, who was still sulking on the edge of the lawn.

"Owl this! Owl that — no one cares about a poor little pussy cat any more," he moaned.

"Of course they do," I whispered. And I picked him up and cuddled him. "I'll always have time for you, Rascal."

He couldn't help himself – as I tickled his ears he began to purr.

"I suppose I can put up with a few feather-brained friends if I have to," he said.

"Of course you can," I giggled. "And you better be nice to them... Or I might just turn you into a slug!"

Aunty Rose came downstairs too, and we stood together watching as the owls disappeared one by one through the little round doorway of their new house.

Little Woo was the last to go inside.

"Twit-woo! Twit-woo!" she called.

"Good night," I whispered under my breath. "Welcome to Honeysuckle Cottage. You'll never want to leave here again. It is the best home anyone could ever have."

Collect the other

Bella Broomstick

books to complete
the series

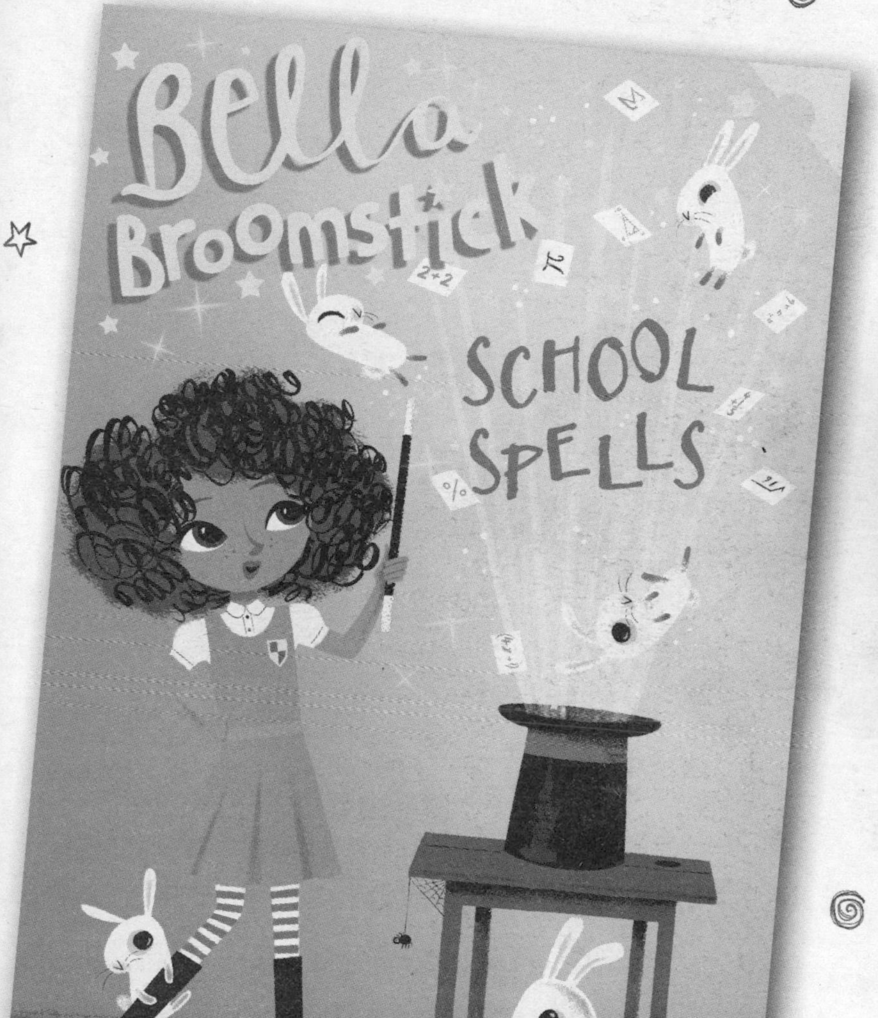

#2

#3

#4

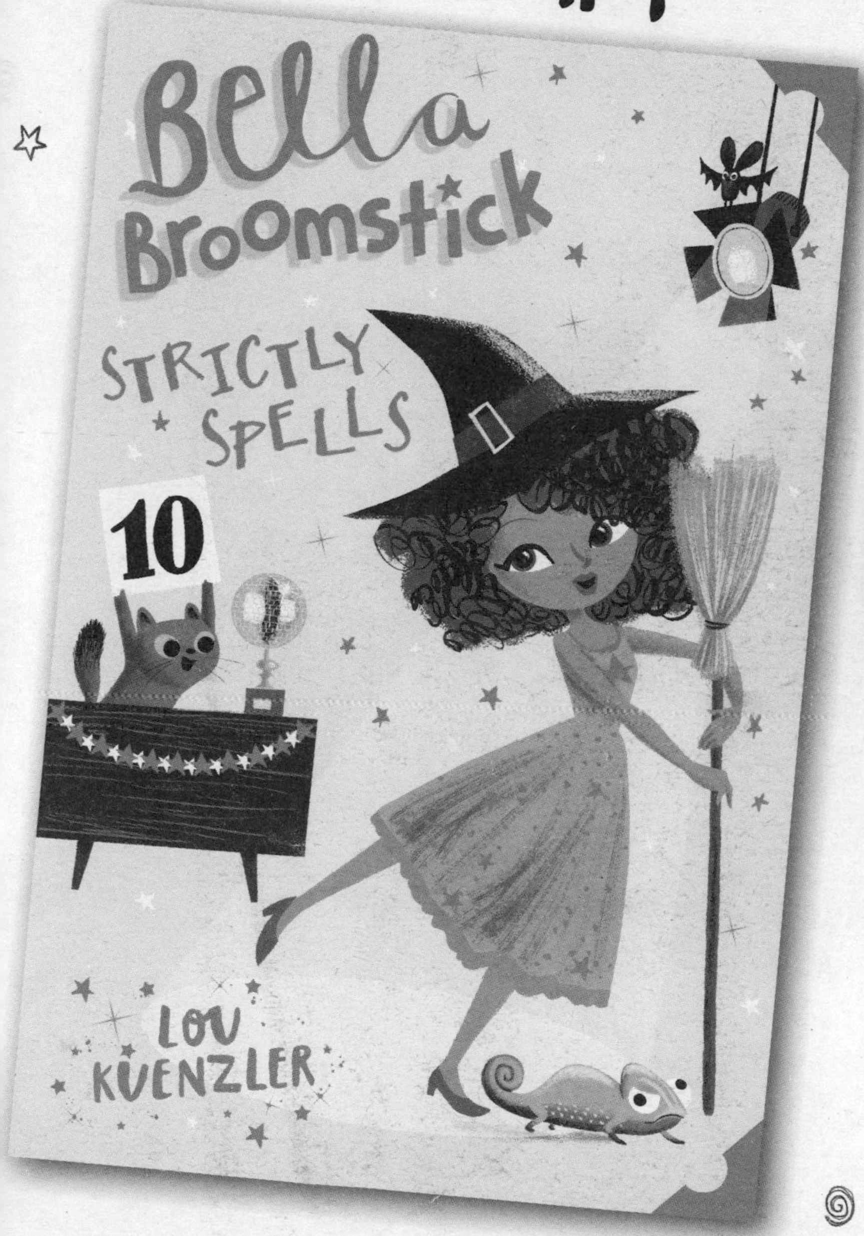

...ty in ... 1972 to prov... ...s and treatment o...ds for ...xampl... f major projects fund...diseases. the Ulverscroft Foundation a...y

- The Children's Eye Unit at Moorf...s Eye Hospital, London
- The Ulverscroft Children's Eye Unit at ...eat Ormond Street Hospital for Sick Children
- Funding research into eye diseases and treatment at the Department of Ophthalmology, University of Leicester
- The Ulverscroft Vision Research Group, Institute of Child Health
- Twin operating theatres at the Western Ophthalmic Hospital, London
- The Chair of Ophthalmology at the Royal Australian College of Ophthalmologists

You can help further the work of the Foundation by making a donation or leaving a legacy. Every contribution is gratefully received. If you would like to help support the Foundation or require further information, please contact:

THE ULVERSCROFT FOUNDATION
The Green, Bradgate Road, Anstey
Leicester LE7 7FU, England
Tel: (0116) 236 4325

website: www.foundation.ulverscroft.com

WITHDRAWN FOR SALE LINCOLNSHIRE COUNTY COUNCIL

04982709

Mari ~~oule~~ was bo~~r~~
Cali~~a~~, of where she h~~a~~
hoo~~d~~ emories of catching ~~t~~apoles
cre~~,~~ picking ripe peaches, and sittin~~g~~
he thinking tree' making up stories. Sh~~e~~
g~~r~~aduated from U.C. Davis with a B.A.
~~A~~fter receiving a Lifetime Teaching Cre-
dential from U.C. Berkeley, she taught art
and math at Rio Americano High School
in Carmichael, La Cumbre Junior High
School in Santa Barbara, and Galesburg-
Augusta High School. She and her
husband live in Michigan, where she
adores the rural beauty, and winter in
Florida.

Visit her website at: marissoule.com